French Fairy Tales

French Fairy Tales

KARA MAY
with illustrations by
MALCOLM ASHMAN

DRAGON'S
WORLD

Dragon's World Ltd
Limpsfield
Surrey RH8 0DY
Great Britain

For IVOR WILLARD
in memory
with love

First published by Dragon's World 1992

© Dragon's World 1992
© Illustrations by Malcolm Ashman 1992
© Text Kara May 1992

Editor   Diana Briscoe
Designer   Judith Robertson
Art Director   Dave Allen
Editorial Director Pippa Rubinstein

British Library Cataloguing in Publication Data
The catalogue record for this book is available from the
British Library.

ISBN 1 85028 206 4

Typeset by Bookworm Typesetting, Manchester, England

Printed in Singapore.

CONTENTS

BEAUTY & THE BEAST

Once a merchant lived in town with his three sons and three daughters. His wife had died but he endeavoured to do the best for his children. He gave them all the good things that money

could buy, including a good education, for he valued knowledge and learning at least as much as his wealth.

The merchant's children all loved him but the youngest was the most devoted. She happily stayed at home with him, as she adored books and music, and her father hired her the best teachers. Not every father took such pains for a daughter and she knew how much she owed him.

Her two elder sisters were equally clever but they were high-spirited, bold, young misses and to stay hidden at home was a bore. They swanned about town in fashionable clothes and proudly paraded their education in witty conversation at parties. And oh how they loved to to be seen in high society. Their sole ambition in life was to reach the top of the social scale. They despised their sister who seemed unable to grasp the importance of money and status and kept company with people who had neither.

'You know nothing of the world,' they sneered. 'You're a stay-at-home blue stocking, Little Sister. What's more, you dress like a frump.'

Maybe her clothes weren't in the latest style, but many people admired

their young sister. Even as a child there was something about her that made them say, 'She's a little beauty.' Now she was older, everyone called her Beauty and her sisters were jealous. 'Our features are as good as hers. Why should they call her "Beauty"?' they secretly raged to each other.

But Beauty seemed to have a light that shone from within. Where it came from they could not tell, but they wished they could take a knife and cut it out of her. Beauty knew her sisters hated her. It wasn't in her heart to bear them malice and she hoped that one day they would love her.

As a rich man's daughters, there was no shortage of men eager to marry them. Beauty felt she was still too young; she wanted to stay at home for a few more years with her father. But she thanked her suitors politely, however, which was more than could be said of her sisters! They jeered at the tradesmen and merchants. Never mind they were merchant's daughters themselves, the haughty young misses declared they'd marry a duke or an earl or no one!

But then, suddenly, the merchant lost all his money and his children's fortunes with it. All he had left was a small farm in the country.

Beauty regretted the loss of her fortune, but she gave no sign of it, not wanting to upset her father. It's gone, she thought, and I must try to be happy without it.

Such a thought never occurred to her sisters. 'The country is for pigs and goats, Papa. We'll choose a husband and stay on in town.'

But now they had no money they found their suitors had vanished. Nor did it help their tempers that Beauty had any number of men still wanting to marry her. But her answer remained the same: she was too young and besides, now she must help her father.

In the country they had to work for a living. Her father and brothers worked in the fields and Beauty would be up at four o'clock to prepare their breakfast. She had the house to see to, the animals to tend and then there was the spinning and weaving.

Her sisters wouldn't deign to dirty their hands. They did nothing but moan how they missed their clever friends and the sophistication of town. All the tasks fell to Beauty. She wasn't used to labouring away like a servant and at first grew pale and thin. But soon she got used to it and her health bloomed – which provoked more taunts from her sisters.

'Only a dolt could thrive in the company of cows and sheep! The country has dulled your mind, Little Sister.'

Their father didn't agree. He found Beauty's company as enjoyable as ever. But he kept his thoughts to himself. He loved all his daughters and didn't want to seem to favour the youngest.

About a year later, he had news that a ship had docked with goods that belonged to him.

'We're rich again, Papa!'

His eldest daughters were thrilled and before he set off for town they gave him a list of things to buy, dresses and hats and other such finery.

The Merchant turned to Beauty. 'And what shall I bring for you?'

Beauty feared her father would have no money left if he bought all the things her sisters had asked for. But she didn't want to make them seem greedy by telling him she wanted nothing. Instead she asked for a rose.

'There are no roses here, Papa. It will be especially precious and rare.'

But when the Merchant got to town there were legal complications and his goods were taken from him. He was as poor as ever and, heavy hearted, he headed for home. And his bad luck was far from over! He got lost in the midst of a forest. It began to snow. He was thrown from his horse and he heard wolves yowling! He feared for his life and how relieved he was to see a light at the end of an avenue of trees. It came from a palace and as he got closer lights appeared in every window.

Thankfully he took his horse to an outlying stable, fed and tethered it and went on to the palace. No one answered his knock but the door opened and he found himself in a vast hall with a welcoming fire in the grate and a splendid meal set out on the table.

The Merchant thought the owner must be coming back shortly and sat down to wait. But when the clock struck eleven, his stomach could wait no longer. The food was delicious and he ate heartily. Now he could think only of bed. Outside it was snowing harder than ever and he was sure the owner wouldn't object if he stayed the night.

After making his way through many lavishly furnished apartments, he came to a bedroom. He slept soundly until morning and when he awoke, he found a fresh suit of clothes laid out beside him. To his surprise, when he looked through the window the snow had gone and the sun now shone on a beautifully tended garden.

There's magic here, he thought. The palace must belong to a Fairy.

He was sure this must be so when he went to the hall and found his breakfast waiting. He said aloud to his magical benefactor, 'Thank you, Ma'am, for your kind hospitality.'

As he went to collect his horse, the Merchant came to a walk with rose trees on either side. He remembered Beauty's request and picked a branch to take home to her. But as soon as the branch was snapped from the tree there was a fearsome noise and standing before him was the most fearsomely ugly creature in a towering rage.

'I saved your life. I tended your every need! And you repay me by stealing my roses, which I value above all else. For this you shall die.'

The Merchant fell to his knees. So this was the owner of the palace, not a fairy after all! 'My lord, forgive me! I meant no offence! I took the roses for my youngest daughter who asked me to bring her one home!'

'Spare me your flattery. You see a Beast and so you shall call me. But you say you have daughters,' went on the Beast. 'I shall pardon you if one of your daughters is prepared to die in your place of her own free will!'

The Merchant began to reply but the Beast cut him short. 'Be on your way. But first, promise you'll return if none of your daughters will die willingly for you.'

The Merchant had no intention of sacrificing one of his daughters to save his own skin. But he would have a chance to say goodbye to his children and so he promised.

'I don't want you going home like a pauper. Go to the room where you slept,' commanded the Beast, 'and there you'll find a chest. Fill it with whatever you please and I'll send on it to you.'

Next to the chest the Merchant found a heap of gold pieces. He filled it to the brim and locked it. At least he'd have something to leave his children. But the Merchant couldn't understand why the Beast should want to kill him on the one hand and give him gifts on the other.

When he got home he gave Beauty the roses. He told her what had happened and the price he must pay for them. Beauty stood as if frozen and said not a word while her sisters wept and turned on her savagely.

'Miss Goody Two Shoes wanted a flower! Too high and mighty to ask for a dress! Your pride has cost dear Papa his life! And you, heartless wretch, can't spare him a tear.'

'Why should I? I propose to return in his place.'

Beauty spoke calmly as if her decision was nothing of consequence.

But her brothers protested they'd sooner kill the Beast or die in the attempt. Their father told them they'd be dead in a trice. 'The Beast has extraordinary powers and you are no match for him. As for your offer Beauty, I appreciate it but I cannot accept it. I'm old and my only regret in dying is parting from my children.'

'When you return to the Beast, I shall come with you. You cannot stop me, Papa, for I shall follow you.'

Her father tried to dissuade her. Beauty was normally open to reason but now she was resolute, 'I have decided, Papa. That's all there is to it.'

Grief-stricken, the Merchant went to his room. He shut the door and jumped as the chest of gold appeared. In all the upset he'd forgotten to

mention it. He decided not to say anything now. His children would want to move back to town but he felt they'd do better to stay in the country, especially without him to look after them.

He confided his secret to Beauty, however. In turn Beauty told him that, during his absence, her sisters had been courted by men who wanted to marry them. 'Give them the money, Papa. Then they can be married in style and live as they please.'

'How can you think of your sisters' comfort when you're about to lose your life? If you insist on coming with me, the Beast is sure to eat us both.'

'I want my sisters to be happy,' said Beauty. 'The rest is my own choice.'

Her sisters were not so caring. When the time came to say goodbye they had to rub their eyes with onions to make them cry, while secretly praying that the Beast would eat her. But her brothers were sincerely sorry to lose her and their tears came from the heart.

Beauty, however, remained dry-eyed. There are tears enough, she thought, without mine.

The horse seemed to know the way to the palace. It led them through the forest, never hesitating where the path divided. Beauty enjoyed the ride to start with; it was a rare treat for her. But soon a terrible fear swept over her and she longed to turn back to the farm where she would be safe.

'Beauty!'

Beauty looked up. Above she saw a figure outlined in light. It was only a glimpse and then it was gone. Had she imagined it? she wondered. Even so, she felt strengthened as they rode on towards the Beast's palace.

As it came into view, Beauty gasped, 'It's magnificent! I had no idea. The Beast must be immensely rich.'

The horse took itself to the stable while Beauty and her father went on into the palace. They found the table set for two in the dining room and their supper laid out for them.

The Beast wants to fatten us up before he eats us! thought Beauty. She had to summon all her will to conceal the terror that churned within her. Her father was so distressed that she forced herself to be cheerful. She chatted brightly as if they were dining at home and persuaded him to eat just a little.

But suddenly there was the fearsome Noise – and there was the Beast. She gazed at him, frozen and filled with horror. Never had she imagined he'd be so grotesque! A Beast indeed!

And yet a part of her pitied him for his awful ugliness.

'Did you come here willingly?' the Beast demanded.

'Y-Y-Yes,' stammered Beauty.

'Then your father may leave in the morning. And now I bid you goodnight.'

As suddenly as he had arrived, the Beast vanished. Her father begged Beauty to flee but her voice was firm and clear as she replied, 'No, Papa. As the Beast said, you shall leave in the morning. You must trust that the Unseen Powers will protect me.'

They were brave words though she was so afraid she was sure she'd never sleep. But her eyes closed as soon as her head touched the pillow.

'Beauty!' It was the same voice she had heard before, and Beauty stirred. Now she saw the figure clearly: it was a Radiant Woman with a light that shimmered about her.

'I am pleased you've chosen to risk your life to save your father's,' the Radiant Woman said. 'Follow this path, Beauty, and you will be rewarded.' Then she vanished. Was it a dream or a vision? Beauty wondered.

She slept peacefully to the next morning. Excitedly she told her father about the Radiant Woman and he agreed that it was a good omen. But he was weeping bitterly as he said goodbye to her.

Beauty watched her father ride away. Now she was alone in the palace. She was sure the Beast would eat her that night. The fear that she'd held at bay for her father's sake swept over her and she wept and wept. But at last, with an effort, she stopped the tears. I'm alive now and I'll enjoy such time as I have, she thought firmly.

She decided to explore the palace. How surprised she was when she came to a door with a sign that said Beauty's Apartment. It was charmingly furnished, exactly to her taste. To her surprise, there was a library and a harpsichord and a collection of music.

Plainly the Beast didn't intend that she should be bored! Then another thought struck her. Surely he wouldn't have gone to such trouble to keep her amused if he planned to eat her that night. She felt even better when she picked up a book that opened by itself at a page that said:

Welcome Beauty, here you are Queen.
Your will and wishes rule supreme.

'What I want now is to see my dear father,' said Beauty.

No sooner had she spoken than she saw her home in the large mirror before her. There was her father, dismounting from his horse, and her brothers and sisters running towards him. The image vanished but now Beauty felt calm enough to explore the library.

At noon she went to the hall and her lunch was waiting. As she ate music played, though she could not tell where it came from. My father was right, she thought. The Beast has remarkable powers and he does seem to want to please me.

But that night, as she sat down to supper, she heard the Noise and the Beast towered before her. Her heart beat like the wings of a terrified bird. How ugly he was! But again a part of her pitied him for it.

For a long while, the Beast just stood, gazing at Beauty. He shifted awkwardly, cleared his throat, made to speak, then paused again.

'May I sit and watch while you eat?' he ventured at last. It was a request, not a command.

Beauty looked up in surprise. 'This is your p-p-palace. It's for you to s-s-say, not me,' she stammered.

'No, you are mistress here. If you want me to go I shall. But tell me truthfully, do you find me ugly?'

'Yes,' whispered Beauty. She was trembling with fear but he'd asked for the truth and she couldn't bring herself to lie.

'I couldn't expect you to find me handsome,' said the Beast 'And my ugliness isn't my only affliction. I'm ignorant, slow-witted! A fool!'

Beauty answered quickly. 'That I doubt, for fools always think they're quite brilliantly clever.'

The Beast seemed at a loss for an answer and took his time to reply. He scratched his head with a puzzled frown and shifted awkwardly from one foot to the other. He's not only ugly, he has no manners or conversation, thought Beauty. But what else could you expect from a Beast? Still that one part of her pitied him.

'I'll come straight to the point,' said the Beast suddenly. 'All I have is yours. I hope you'll enjoy living here. My one wish is for you to be happy.'

The words were more grunted at her than spoken, but Beauty saw that he meant them and her fear of him all but left her.

'Your kindness is very pleasing to me, Beast. I thank you for it. Indeed, as I look at you now, I can almost forget that you're ugly.'

'Oh, yes, I have a good enough heart. But to the world, I'm a monster.'

'From what I know of the world there are many who deserve the name more.' said Beauty. 'I prefer you to those who are corrupt, cruel or greedy.'

'If I were clever,' the Beast said, 'I could make a gracious reply. As it is I can only say Thank you and ask, Will you be my wife?'

The proposal took her unawares. Beauty recoiled in horror and shock. If she refused, would he turn angry and eat her? It took all her courage to answer, 'I do not love you, Beast. I cannot be your wife.'

The Beast gave a sigh so anguished that the vast hall couldn't contain it and it echoed all around the palace. But he made no attempt to harm her. 'I shall leave you to finish your meal in peace. Goodnight, Beauty.'

Before he left the hall, he turned back for another sight of her. Poor Beast, she thought. He's so kind but so ugly no one will want to marry him.

Three months passed. Beauty had nothing to do but amuse herself with books and music or enjoy the garden with its glorious abundance of flowers. Her meals appeared ready made for her. Silk dresses filled her wardrobe. She had only to say, 'I'd like a dish of fresh raspberries' or 'It would be pleasant to hear some music,' and the raspberries would be there in an instant and music would fill the air. And if she wanted to know what was happening at home, the magic mirror would show her.

She never saw the Beast during the day. But every evening, as she sat down to supper, the Beast would arrive. He never ate with her, but he urged her to talk of whatever she chose. He was happy to listen but once when he tried to speak himself, he broke off in angry despair, 'I'm boring and dull! I'm an ignorant oaf!'

'You're not an oaf,' Beauty cried, 'You are kindness itself. You're ignorant because you have no education, but I can teach you.'

With Beauty's help, the Beast began to study and improve his mind. It was an effort and his conversation was still more plodding than brilliant. But he had his own good common sense and Beauty found she enjoyed his company. In fact she could hardly wait for the hour when he would arrive.

But one thing still distressed her. He would always ask her to marry him before he said goodnight. At last she decided she must tell him clearly she could never be his wife.

'I don't want you to hope that I'll ever feel otherwise,' she said. 'I like you! You are my dear Beast and my friend. Please, be content with that.'

'If I must, I must. I can't blame you if you can't love me, I'm all too aware of my shortcomings. But I love you. I'll be happy as long as you're here. Promise, Beauty, you'll never leave me.'

Beauty blushed. She had been thinking of doing just that! She'd watched in the magic mirror as her sisters got married and her brothers joined the army. Now her father was ill and missing her terribly.

'If you'd let me visit him, dear Beast, I could promise not to leave you for long. If you refuse I fear I shall fret, perhaps to my death!' said Beauty.

The Beast protested that he'd send her home sooner than let her suffer a moment's unhappiness. 'Forget your poor Beast. He shall die of grief.'

'Don't say such a thing!' Beauty burst into tears. 'Now look! You've made me cry. I shall return in a week, I promise.'

The Beast told her she'd be with her father next morning and begged her not to forget her promise. Then he gave her a ring. 'When you're ready to return, put it on your bedside table. It will bring you back to me.'

The Beast sighed that sigh that never failed to touch her heart with its sorrow. Beauty made her way to her bedroom, sad that she couldn't love him as he wished.

The next morning she woke to find herself in her own bed in her father's house. She rang for the maid who was startled out of her wits! Her father came running and was overjoyed to see his daughter.

Beauty got up to dress, then she realised she'd no clothes to wear. But at that moment the maid came bursting back in, agog with wonder. 'I tell no word of a lie, Miss, but a chest come flying into the room next door and it's full of dresses as you've never seen, all covered with gold and diamonds!'

Even apart from her, her Beast was as thoughtful as ever. The least she could do, thought Beauty, was to wear one of the gowns he'd troubled to send her. She chose the plainest, though it was still exceptionally beautiful.

'I'll give the others to my sisters, Papa,' she said

Her father laughed as the chest vanished. 'I think the Beast means the clothes are for you, not your sisters.'

'I think you must be right!' said Beauty as the chest swiftly returned.

She couldn't wait to send word to her sisters that she was home and longing to see them. They soon arrived with their husbands but how unhappy they were!

Her eldest sister had married a man who was stunningly handsome, but so much in love with himself that he had no love left for his wife. The second sister had a husband who was dazzlingly clever, but he used his searing wit to point out the failings of the world at large and those of his unfortunate wife in particular. Her sisters were in no mood to enjoy seeing Beauty dressed like a princess and obviously enjoying her life at the palace where, it seemed, her wishes and will counted for everything.

More than ever before they were ravaged by jealousy. They went off to the garden to plot against their sister. They decided to lavish pretended love on her to persuade her to stay for more than a week. They hoped that the Beast would be so angry she'd broken her promise, that he'd eat her.

What a show they put on! It was, 'Dear Beauty, this', 'Dear Beauty that'. When the week was up, they wept and said they would die if she left. Thinking they loved her at last, Beauty agreed to stay a week longer.

Ten days had passed since she'd left the Beast. She couldn't help thinking of how much he'd have missed her. And I miss him too, thought Beauty.

It took her a long time to sleep that night. But at last she drifted into a dream. In the dream she saw the canal that ran through the gardens of the palace. Lying on the bank was the Beast. How thin he looked, how pale! His voice was the faintest whisper. 'Beauty,' he said, 'I gave you all you desired, but you broke your promise and I shall die of it.'

Beauty woke with a start. It was only a dream, but it was true she'd broken her promise. If the Beast were to suffer on her account, she'd never forgive herself. She should have said that she would marry him. It wasn't his fault he was ugly and not very clever. His heart was true and he loved her. I'm not in love with him, but what of it! I like and respect him, thought Beauty. At least she would be happier than her sisters. Their husbands might be handsome and clever, but they were also unfeeling and cold.

She put the ring on the bedside table and, when she woke the next morning, she was overjoyed to find herself back at the palace. Light-hearted, she chose the loveliest of the gowns the Beast had given her. Then she waited impatiently for the hour when he always arrived. But the hour came and went without a sign of him.

Distraught, she searched the palace. Then she remembered her dream and ran into the garden. She found the Beast by the bank of the canal, ghostly pale and still. 'He's dead. I'm too late!' cried Beauty.

In a torrent of tears she held him close. It was then she felt his heart beating. Quickly she fetched some water and trickled it over his head.

At last the Beast opened his eyes. 'You forgot your promise, Beauty. I vowed I'd starve rather than live without you. But now I shall die happy.'

'Forgive me, dear Beast, I've been so stupid!' cried Beauty. 'I thought I valued you just as a friend. But I was wrong. I love you! I promise to marry you. You must live and be my husband.'

As she said this, the palace was suddenly ablaze with light. Fireworks burst into the sky and music filled the air.

Beauty looked about her in terror. 'My dear Beast, what is happening?'

But the Beast had vanished. Kneeling at her feet was a handsome prince who thanked her for releasing him from the spell which had cursed him for so long. He said that a Fairy had turned him into a beast, blocked his mind of its cleverness and decreed he'd remain a stupid beast unless a beautiful girl promised to marry him. 'The Fairy left me one asset, a generous heart. Only you, Beauty, were wise enough to love me for it.'

The Prince presented Beauty with his crown. 'Nothing I can give you can repay the debt that I owe you.'

Together they went into the palace. To Beauty's astonishment, there was her father and her sisters. Then, coming towards her, she saw a figure circled with light. It was the Radiant Woman who said, 'You thought I was a dream, Beauty, but I've always been with you.'

Beauty was too awed to speak. She could only listen, wondering, as the Radiant Woman went on, 'I applaud your choice of a husband. You have chosen a good heart, rather than brains or good looks and I reward you with a Prince who has all three. You will be a great Queen and rule wisely.

'As for you,' the Radiant Woman turned to the elder sisters, 'I decree that your pride and greed shall imprison you in stone. You shall stand as statues in your sister's palace and witness her happiness. Perhaps one day your vices will change to virtues. It will take time, but it is not impossible.'

The Radiant Woman waved her wand. In that moment they were all taken to the Prince's kingdom, where his subjects greeted them with joy. Beauty and the Prince were married and they lived together in happiness that lasted ever after.

THE LITTLE GLASS SLIPPER

There are some men who are loving, fearless and brave. There are others who are kind-hearted enough in their way, but as gutless and spineless as a jellyfish. The Nobleman in this story was definitely one of the latter.

The Nobleman's wife adored him, however, and he knew he was lucky to have her. She was young and beautiful, and did everything for him. So much so that, when she died, he could scarcely tie his own shoelaces, let alone look after himself and his daughter.

I must find a new wife at once! he decided. If she was rich, so much the better (he had lost his own money long since)!

He married a rich widow with two daughters.

In his second marriage, the Nobleman wasn't so fortunate. His new wife was haughty and proud: the last thought in her mind was to run round after him. She had money, yes! But she was so tightfisted, she'd drink his blood sooner than spend it.

And that wasn't the worst of it! Far from mothering his beloved young daughter, his new wife made her the castle maid-of-all-work.

The poor girl had to sleep in the attic while her step-sisters slept in her cosy bedroom. When she wasn't slaving away, the Nobleman's daughter had to stay in the kitchen. It was cold and drafty, so she sat in the hearth in the cinders to keep warm. But even then she had no peace! Her step-sisters, full of airs and graces, came swanning down to make fun of her.

'Ladies sit on chairs, not in the cinders,' they jeered.

'You're just a kitchen maid, a slavey,' jeered the elder.

The younger, never quite so cruel, contented herself with chanting, 'You're a Little Cinders! You're a Cinderella!'

Just as Cinderella took after her mother, her new sisters took after theirs. Pride twisted their mouths into corkscrews and their eyes were piglike with venom and spite. They were always in a rage about something, and they seemed to like nothing and no-one – not even each other. Certainly they had no love for their new step-father's daughter.

It was a real puzzle to Cinderella why her step-sisters hated her, for she waited on them from dawn to dusk and did her best to please them.

But though they'd sooner die than admit it, her step-sisters hated her because she was beautiful. Cinderella had a beauty that shone through in the light of her eyes and the warmth of her smile. Even barefoot and in rags, she outshone them. It made her step-sisters seethe with a jealous rage and they made her life a torment. Day in and day out it was: PINCH! SLAP!

'Do this, Slavey!'

'Do that, Cinderella!'

Her father knew what was going on, but he shut himself up in his study and Cinderella had to put up with it. She never thought to complain. She knew that he loved her, but she knew the sort of man he was, that he was too scared of his wife to stick up for her. Her father was as he was, she thought, and there was no point in wishing him otherwise.

Then a day came when Cinderella wished, as never before, that she could take her place as her father's daughter instead of the castle drudge.

One morning an envelope arrived bearing the royal crest. In the envelope was an invitation from the Prince who was giving a two-night ball at the palace.

Cinderella's sisters, for once, stopped scowling; their faces lit up with delight.

'I shall dance with the Prince! What bliss!' sighed the elder.

'You might dance with the Prince! But I'll be the one he takes to supper! What ecstasy!' purred the younger.

Cinderella too was aglow with excitement. To go the palace in all its splendour! To dance! To feast at the royal table! And to see for herself if the Prince was as good-natured and handsome as rumour would have it!

But her name wasn't on the invitation.

'Of course it's not! Only ladies are invited!' scoffed the younger.

'Not little kitchen maids!' sneered the elder.

Morning, noon and night her sisters talked of the BALL at the PALACE. Above all, they talked about what they should wear. (They'd have liked something new, but they knew better than to ask their mother!)

'I'll wear my red velvet,' the elder decided. 'I'll dress it up with Honiton lace, while you have to make do with that old skirt!' she sneered down at her nose at the younger.

'Maybe I will!' the younger retorted. 'But I've got my top with the diamonds on it. And my gold-flowered shawl! At the very least, I'll look a hundred times better than you!'

'No you won't!'

'Yes I will!'

That set them off, screeching and scratching. Then they turned on Cinderella: PINCH! SLAP!

'Iron my dress, you lazy Slavey!'

'Wash my skirt! Now! At once!'

At last the day of the first ball arrived. 'You must help us get ready,' her step-sisters demanded.

Cinderella wasn't just useful at washing and ironing! She had a flair for making them look their best.

'Do my hair first!' screeched the elder.

'You're always first!' yelled the younger.

They flung themselves at each other in a fearsome rage. PINCH! SLAP!

'It's your fault we're fighting, Cinders.'

'If you weren't such a clodhead, you could do my hair and my sister's together!'

'She's jealous!'

'Jealous because she can't come to the ball!'

The elder smiled oh-so-sweetly. 'Would you like to come with us, Slavey?'

Cinderella's heart leapt. 'Why yes! I would love to!'

Her step-sisters shrieked with laughter.

'I was only joking, you little dolt!'

'As if they'd let a Cinders like you into the palace!'

Cinderella had curling tongs in her hand. She could have scorched her sisters' hair, she could have made them look perfect frights! But she just silently sighed and curled their hair and made them look their prettiest.

They were admiring themselves in the mirror when the coach arrived.

'See you later, Slavey!' said the elder.

'We're off to the ball! Lucky us!'

Off they went to the palace with their mother and step-father, while Cinderella sat by the kitchen hearth, all alone in the castle.

It wasn't often she cried but now the tears flowed swift and fast.

'Cinderella!'

Cinderella looked up to see a woman hovering in the air before her.

'I'm your Fairy Godmother,' she said. 'Tell me child, what is the matter?'

'I wish…. I wish….'

But Cinderella was sobbing so hard she couldn't get the words out.

The Fairy smiled. 'Like all Fairy Godmothers, I can read your heart. You wish to go to the ball, and so you shall. Go into the garden and fetch me a pumpkin.'

How a pumpkin could help her go to the ball, Cinderella couldn't imagine. But she did as the Fairy instructed.

'Watch, Cinderella!' The Fairy tapped the pumpkin with her ring. And there instead of a pumpkin was a coach, a most magnificent coach.

'What we need now are horses to pull it. See if there are any mice in the mouse-trap.'

Cinderella found six mice, all alive and bright-eyed. The Fairy tapped them with her ring and they turned into fine dapple-grey horses, a little mousey in colour, but strong and sleek.

'We have the coach and the horses!' said the Fairy. 'But who shall drive them? Where is our coachman?'

Inspired by the Fairy's example, Cinderella suggested, 'Shall I see if there's a rat in the rat-trap?'

There were three rats in the trap. One had long bristly whiskers. The Fairy touched him with her magic ring, and there was a burly coachman with a curling moustache.

'Go into the garden once more, my dear,' said the Fairy, 'and bring me six lizards. You'll find them behind the watering can!'

A touch of the magic ring and the six lizards became six footmen in gold braided coats. 'They'll escort you to the ball. Now off you go,' said the Fairy.

Cinderella hesitated. She was dressed in rags and her feet were bare.

'Am I to go the ball as I am?'

'Since you ask, no, child. Come here.'

Cinderella stepped forward and the Fairy touched her once with her ring. The rags vanished and in their place was a dress of silk that shimmered with threads of gold and silver and her feet were shod in the daintiest pair of glass slippers.

'Now you are ready. Off you go, Cinderella! But first, let me give you a warning. You must leave before midnight. At midnight the magic will fade and you will be left as you were, in rags and tatters.'

Promising to leave well before that, Cinderella set off for the ball.

When the glittering coach arrived at the palace, word was sent to the Prince that a princess had arrived. He ran down to greet her and a flame

seemed to light in his heart as his eyes fell on Cinderella, a-shimmer in a gown that outshone all others and looking oh so beautiful.

He led her into the ballroom to oohs's and aah's of admiration. Even the old King remarked to the Queen that it was a long time since he'd seen a girl of such grace and beauty. They were not at all surprised when their son would dance with nobody else and chose to take 'the princess' in to supper.

Cinderella was enraptured by the Prince's attention. But even so, family was family. She excused herself and joined her sisters, offering to share the dish of oranges and lemons which the Prince himself had given her.

To her astonishment her sisters didn't know who she was. But there was no time to explain! It was already a quarter to midnight. Cinderella hurried away and managed to get back home on the last stroke of midnight.

As her Fairy Godmother had warned, the magic vanished. There she was in her rags with a pumpkin, six mice, a rat and six lizards.

She began to wonder if she'd been to the ball, perhaps she'd dreamt it! But then her sisters arrived, full of talk of the beautiful princess.

'And guess who she choose to talk to!'

'Guess who she shared her oranges and lemons with, served by the Prince himself!'

'Us!' shrieked her sisters, bursting with triumph.

Cinderella could hardly contain her delight. She gave a mischievous smile. 'Who was she, this "Princess"?'

'Nobody knows. But the Prince said he'd give the world to find out.'

'Perhaps she'll be there tomorrow. I'd love to see her.' Cinderella turned to her elder sister. 'Would you lend me your yellow dress, the one you wear every day? Then I could go to the ball.'

'You could if I would, but I won't!' was her sister's reply.

Cinderella was rather relieved. For the Prince to see her dressed like a princess was one thing! For him to see her in her sister's old gown was another!

All night she tossed and turned, wondering if her Fairy Godmother would help her once more to go to the ball. But the next evening, as soon as her family had left, the Fairy arrived and sent her off to the palace in a gown even more soft, silky and shimmering than her gown of the night before.

'But remember what will happen when midnight strikes,' warned the Fairy.

'I'll leave well before then,' said Cinderella.

When she saw the Prince, when she saw how his face lit up at the sight of her, Cinderella found her heart beating quite as fast as his! Her head was awhirl as they danced together. She lost all thought of her sisters, all thought of the time – until the clock began to strike midnight.

With a startled cry, Cinderella fled from the ballroom towards the stairs. The Prince ran after her, but she was too quick for him. She slipped out of the door and vanished into the night.

'What a fool I am!' raged the Prince. 'I quite forgot to ask where she came from or even her name!'

With a heavy heart, he turned back up the stairs. Then he spied the little glass slipper which his 'princess' had dropped in her haste, lying on a step half way down the stairs. He picked it up and declared: 'Whomsoever this slipper fits, I shall marry!'

His parents were horrified. 'That slipper could fit anyone, not just your Princess!'

But the Prince was adamant. 'Be that as it may, if I cannot marry my Princess, I shall marry the girl who can wear her slipper.' And the next morning he sent a footman to tour the land with the glass slipper.

Cinderella's sisters waited their turn in a state of frenzied impatience. (The duchesses and other grand ladies were to have their turn first.) They could neither eat nor sleep and they squabbled more fiercely than ever.

'I've a much better a chance than you,' crowed the elder. 'My feet are remarkably small!'

'Remarkably small and remarkably fat!' snapped the younger.

'At least they're not as long as a rake and covered in bunions!'

'I might have bunions but I haven't got corns!'

And so it went on.

But at last came the KNOCK! at the door. There was the Prince's footman bearing a cushion, and on the cushion was the little glass slipper that brought the prospect of the Prince for a husband.

The elder pushed the younger aside and grabbed it. But squeeze as she might her foot was too fat and when the younger's turn came, hers was too long. They tried again and again. If their lives had depended on it, they couldn't have struggled harder to get their feet into that slipper.

Cinderella was tempted to laugh but they looked so very desperate, it would have been too unkind.

'May I try?' she ventured at last.

'You! What a nerve! What a cheek!' stormed her sisters.

'Every unmarried woman in the land must try it on. By order of the Prince!' said the Footman.

Cinderella's heart was beating fast. She knew the slipper would fit. But now the Prince would know who she was. Not a princess! But Cinders, the castle drudge.

Trembling, she put on the slipper. It slipped on to her foot, a perfect fit. From her apron pocket, she took the other. 'Here is its partner,' she said.

Her sisters were half in a faint and the Footman was so surprised that his chin dropped on to his chest.

They were even more astonished when the Fairy appeared. 'Now the world shall see you for who you are, Cinderella.'

She tapped Cinderella with her ring and her rags dissolved into a gown that shone and shimmered.

Her sisters started, pale and aghast. 'The Princess! It was you!' They'd sat with her at the ball but they hadn't known her, their own sister!

They were filled with shame and remorse.

'I've been such a pig. Will you ever forgive me Cinders? I mean…. er…. um….' sobbed the elder.

'You can pull my hair and slap me as hard as you like! It's no less than I deserve!' wept the younger.

Cinderella, who hadn't thought about vengeance before, wasn't going to start now! She hugged her sisters, then she drove off in the coach to the palace.

When the Prince saw her, he felt his heart would burst with happiness and they planned to marry three days later.

But there was to be more than one marriage that day! Cinderella knew only too well how cheerless life was at the castle. If her step-sisters could be happily married, they would be the happier for it, and so would she.

Two handsome young men, one a marquis and the other an earl, had noted the sisters at the ball (laughing and happy for once, instead of scowling!). They were glad to offer their hands in marriage to the new princess's step-sisters, and were very gladly accepted. The three sisters were married together and such celebrations had never been seen in the land before.

Now with the daughters gone, Cinderella's father and his wife were alone in the cold crumbling castle with no company but each other's. What became of them? Well, that's another story.

THE KINDLY FROG

This is a story of a time long ago, a time of extraordinary happenings and magical beings, some good and some evil. It is also the story of a Queen, a King, a Princess and a Prince.

Imagine a city, the capital city of a country which has been at war with its neighbours for many years. The enemy has surrounded the city and the King and Queen are besieged with their people.

THE QUEEN

The King and the Queen loved each other but they didn't agree about everything. Despite the danger that threatened, the Queen wanted to stay in the city. But the King wanted her to flee to a secret fortress. Few people knew where to find it – even he had been there just once – and there she would be safe. The Queen begged him not to send her away, she'd sooner die at his side than be parted from him. But the King wouldn't listen. He told his guards to take the Queen to the fortress and keep her there till the war was over.

'I'll visit you if I can,' he said. (There wasn't much hope of him getting away but he hoped that it would make her feel better.)

The fortress lay in a wasteland in the middle of a dense forest. There was nothing to do and no friends to amuse her. 'The King says he loves me yet he sends me to this dreary place! I'll die of boredom!' wailed the Queen.

She was angry. But even more, she was upset to think of her husband facing the perils of war without her. And she missed him terribly. At last she could stand it no longer.

I shall return to the city, the Queen decided. She'd have to find her own way, but an Unseen Power had always protected her and she trusted it would guide her now. She began to plot her escape.

First the Queen told the guards she wanted to join them when they went hunting. 'I want you to make me a chariot ,' she said, 'so I can keep up with the hounds.' Cleverly she had the chariot built to take only one person, so she would have to drive it. The Queen selected the horses too, fiery steeds that could outrun all the others.

'Now let a hunt be held!' she commanded.

Rather than hunting clothes, the Queen chose a dress with precious stones all over the front and a hat with tall feathers of every colour. Soon she would be with her husband, and she wanted to look her most beautiful.

When the hunt set off the Queen told everyone to follow a different path so the quarry wouldn't escape. Alone at last she urged on her horses.

The horses seemed to have a will of their own. They galloped faster, faster, faster. She tried to restrain them but they were too strong for her.

What a fool she'd been to think she could manage them! If only she'd stayed in the fortress!

She called on the Unseen Power, to the fairies and the sacred beings of the forest to come to her aid. But she called in vain and the horses sped on, still faster and faster. Suddenly the chariot swerved. The Queen saw what was coming. She jumped, but not quite quickly enough. Her foot caught between the wheel and its axle as the chariot crashed to the ground.

Certain that she had passed from the Land of the Living into the Realm of the Dead, warily the Queen opened her eyes.

A gigantic woman towered over her. All she wore was a lion's skin, her arms and legs were bare. Her mane of hair was tied with the skin of a snake whose head dangled over her shoulder. Over her other shoulder was a quiver of arrows and in one hand she held a stone club.

'No wonder they say you need courage to die if the Realm of the Dead holds such horrors as this!' the Queen murmured.

The Giantess overheard her. 'You're not in the Realm of the Dead! There's plenty of life in you yet. But you'll need all your courage. I am the Lion-Witch and you're coming to live with me.'

The Queen begged her to let her go. 'My husband loves me. He'll reward you richly.'

'I've wealth enough of my own, I don't need your husband's! But I'm weary of living alone,' said the Lion-Witch, 'and you could prove useful – if you keep your wits about you! But there's no place for finery, not in my realm! Leave your fancy dress here, and your fancy hat.'

Before the Queen's terrified gaze, the Lion-Witch turned herself into a lioness. She flung the Queen over her shoulder and carried her down six thousand steps to the deepest bowels of the earth.

'This is my realm,' she said.

The only light came from a lake of quicksilver. The water heaved with monsters that wriggled and writhed. Above the wings of ravens and screech-owls and other birds of ill-omen flapped; their spine-chilling cries filled the foul-smelling air.

In the distance the Queen saw a mountain. But there was nothing to comfort her here. The trees had neither fruits nor leaves and the ground was a wildness of nettles and briars. Down the barren slopes inched a sludgy stream.

To the Queen's dismay the Lion-Witch told her it was watered by the tears of unhappy lovers. Then she pointed to a clump of horse-chestnuts, withered roots and thorn apples. 'That's your breakfast, lunch and tea. Not what you're used to, but it's all that you'll get. Now we shall go to my lair.'

The Lion-Witch's lair was deep in a cavern. There was only the ground to sleep on, it was cold and comfortless. The Queen shivered. This was worse than the fortress!

To her surprise however, fierce as she was, the Lion-Witch revealed remarkable powers of healing and quickly healed her terrible wounds.

But the Queen had no chance to rest.

'There are no servants here,' said the Lion-Witch. 'You'll do your own work, you're strong enough now. To begin with, you can build yourself a hut. And make a good job of it. You'll be here for the rest of your life.'

'For the rest of my life!' The Queen turned pale and burst into tears. 'If I'm never to see my husband again, kill me now! Put an end to my misery.'

The Lion-Witch raised her hefty stone-club. 'Stop your weeping! You'll do as I say or be the worse for it.'

'Is there nothing I can do,' implored the terrified Queen, 'that would soften your heart towards me?'

'I've a liking for fly pasties. But I warn you. I like them large, thick and juicy with flies.'

The Queen protested there were no flies there! Besides, there wasn't enough light to catch them by. 'And I've never made a pasty in all my life.'

'What I want, I shall have!' roared the Lion-Witch. 'Don't let me see you again without one that will fill my hand.'

The Queen didn't bother to reply. Nor did she attempt to hunt for flies. What was the point? The task was impossible. If she kills me, so be it, she thought. This place is so awful that death would be a release. If I'm never to see my darling husband again, it's nothing to me to die.

The thought of her husband fuelled her despair. He was sure to think she was dead. How distraught he would be without her. But for how long? she wondered. In time he'd forget her and marry another.

This made her feel even more wretched. But she was startled out of her misery by the screech of a raven. In its beak was a frog. At any moment the bird would devour it.

Quickly the Queen picked up a stick. 'I can't help myself, but at least I can save the poor little frog!' She turned on the raven and forced it to let go of its prey.

The Frog lay stunned on the ground. Then something quite extraordinary happened. It began to speak in a voice that was sweet and clear as crystal.

'O Queen most beautiful, since I came here,' said the Frog 'you're the first person to befriend me.'

'What power has given you the gift of speech?' the Queen gasped.

'I am part fairy,' the Frog replied.

'Then why did you come to this terrible place?'

'My curiosity brought me.'

'And who are these other people? I've not met anyone since I arrived.'

The Frog pointed to the monsters in the Lake of Quicksilver. 'Once they were kings and queens, tyrants who caused their people bloodshed and strife. Later they'll return to the world. But their natures are such, they'll return none the better or wiser.'

'Keeping wicked people together isn't likely to improve them, I can see that,' said the Queen. 'But at least one day they'll be free. I'm to stay here forever.'

They saw the raven hovering above. The Fairy explained that her 0power lay in her magic cap of roses. She had left it by the marshes and it was then the bird had pounced. 'If it weren't for you, gracious Queen, I'd have been eaten alive.'

They hastened to fetch the cap of roses.

'In some things, though not in all, it gives me limitless power.' said the Frog. 'But I'll help as I best I can to lighten your miserable life here.'

'Thank you, dear, dear Frog. But I'm beyond helping. The Lion-Witch has set me an impossible task. If she doesn't get what she wants,' wept the Queen, 'I'm as good as dead. She's likely to club me to death.'

She explained about the fly pasty.

'Leave that to me!' said the Frog.

She summoned six thousand frogs. Next she smeared herself all over with sugar and instructed them to do the same. Then she led them to a secret place where the Lion-Witch had a store of flies which she released from time to time to torment her unfortunate victims.

The flies smelt the sugar and flew at the frogs, and stuck. The Queen gathered them up and shaped them into a pasty! It was a messy, sticky business, but she managed it.

'How did you do it?' demanded the Lion-Witch. 'Some Unseen Power must have assisted you.'

The Queen answered vaguely, 'You wanted the pasty and so I made it.'

For the moment, the Lion-Witch left her in peace. But she wouldn't let her into her lair to escape the poisonous fumes that rose from the lake. I'd best build a hut, the Queen decided. She hadn't just herself to think of now; she had just realised she was carrying a child.

She cut some branches from the ever-green cypress. The Frog and her friends came to help, and soon the hut was finished. It was snug and cosy. Thankfully the Queen lay down to rest. But not for long! The monsters of the lake began to howl. Jealous of the Queen's cosy dwelling, they were determined to drive her out of it. They made such a din, the Queen feared she'd go mad. She fled from the hut and a monster, once a tyrant king, moved into it.

'That's not fair!' protested the Queen.

The monsters laughed and jeered. So the Queen complained to the Lion-Witch. She found no sympathy there: 'Don't come bleating to me unless you want a thrashing!'

The Queen told the Frog what had happened. The Frog could weep like a mortal, and they both wept. 'Never mind the monsters,' said the Frog at last. 'I'll build you something better than a hut – a country mansion away from the lake where they cannot reach it.'

With the help of her frog-assistants she cut some wood and soon the the house was finished. It was pretty and charming with every home-comfort. There was even a bed of sweet thyme to sleep on.

Again the Lion-Witch demanded, 'Who is the Unseen Power who assists you? No herbs grow here, none that I know of, not even the hardy sage.'

Again the Queen was evasive. 'Perhaps it's the child that I'm carrying. I hope,' she added, 'its destiny will be more fortunate than mine.'

'I don't want to hear about you. I want some flowers. A posy of exotic flowers! Let us see if your child can help you again!' said the Lion-Witch.

Flowers? thought the Queen. In this place? That never sees the light of day, let alone the light of the sun?

'She must know that it's impossible! Dear Frog, what shall I do!' sobbed the Queen.

'My friend, the Bat, can help you. She moves more swiftly than I,' said the Frog. 'I'll lend her my cap of roses to guide her to the secret places where exotic flowers grow.'

The kindly Frog summoned the Bat and a few hours later the Bat returned with a posy of exquisite flowers of all colours.

Now the Lion-Witch was certain that some Unseen Power was helping the Queen. But whomsoever it was, this was her realm and her power was the greater: the Queen would remain her prisoner.

The Queen, however, was forever dreaming up plans of escape and she told the Frog how much she missed her husband.

'I'll confer with my cap of roses and see what it advises. But first I must perform the ritual.'

The Frog made a fire of straw and burnt two green peas, juniper twigs and capers. She croaked five times, then the words of the oracle flowed smoothly through her as if spun on a silver thread:

'Fate, all powerful and wise, decrees that you, O Queen, from the World above, shall remain below in the realm of the Lion-Witch and here give birth to your child.

'Your child shall be be a daughter and she shall be as fair as Aphrodite, the Goddess of Love herself. Now be at peace. Only time will heal. I have spoken.'

Soon after, as the Frog predicted, the Queen gave birth to a daughter who was indeed extraordinarily beautiful. But the Queen's joy was all too brief. The Lion-Witch demanded the newborn princess, saying she wanted to eat her.

Now it was the Queen who was fierce. Fiercely she argued and pleaded to be allowed to keep her child, and at last the Lion-Witch agreed.

The Queen called the princess Moufette. What a treasure she was! How the King would love her. But the King didn't know about her. And by now, thought the Queen, he'll have forgotten me and found a new wife.

Even more than before, it was a thought that pricked at her heart like a hot needle. As the years passed, she couldn't dislodge it.

Her anguish touched the Frog so deeply that she offered to seek out the King and tell him the Queen was alive and where she was. 'I'm a slow traveller, but sooner or later I'll find him.'

The Queen was overjoyed. But then another thought troubled her. 'The King could never rescue me, not from here. Why tell him where I am?'

'We must do what we are able,' said the Frog, 'and leave the rest to fate.'

Without evidence, the Queen feared her husband wouldn't believe what the Frog told him. But he knew her handwriting and she decided to write him a letter to prove she was indeed alive.

She had neither paper nor ink but she wasn't deterred: for paper, she used a scrap of rag; for ink, she used her own blood.

Sadly the Queen watched the Frog depart. Now she would have to fend for herself and her daughter without the help of her benevolent friend. Eagerly she awaited the Frog's return. But the years passed and the Queen did her best to look after her daughter. She had feared the harsh life in the

realm of the Lion-Witch would make her daughter sullen and sour. But the Princess bloomed.

Her extraordinary beauty drove the monsters into a frenzy of love and they threw themselves at her feet. Terrified, the Princess fled to the protective arms of her mother. She'd known the monsters all her life but never lost her fear of them.

'This place is dreadful, Mother!' she cried. 'Must we stay here forever?'

The Queen, too, was deeply despairing. But she rallied her spirits for the sake of her daughter.

'We are better off than we were,' she said. 'Now that the Lion-Witch takes us hunting, we have a glimpse of the world above.'

The Lion-Witch had a liking to feed on rabbits and other creatures not found in her realm. In her lioness form she carried the Queen and the Princess on her back up into the forest and taught them to hunt. They were only allowed the head or feet of their kill to eat but they saw the light of day for a few hours!

'And remember the Frog,' said the Queen to her daughter. 'Perhaps she'll find her way to the King. Then who knows what may happen.'

So many years had passed, the Queen had all but given up hope of the Frog returning with news of the King. Even so, a forlorn hope was better than none.

THE KING

And what of the King? Had he survived the war? And if he had, had he married again as the Queen feared? What had happened was this:

The King drove his enemies out of his kingdom. Triumphantly he went to fetch the Queen from the fortress. There the guards told him they had found the Queen's chariot, horses and bloodstained clothes in the forest. But they'd found no sign of the Queen herself.

The King thought his wife had been eaten by wolves. He went half mad with grief. He blamed himself for sending her away. She hadn't wanted to go and, if he'd listened to her, she'd still be alive.

Heart-broken, he returned to the city. He declared that peace should now reign in his kingdom and he released his subjects from military service. His former enemies befriended him and offered their condolences.

For fourteen years the King grieved for the Queen and the land was overcast with gloom and despair. His subjects begged him to marry again, the country needed an heir. At last the King yielded and agreed to marry a Princess who was young and agreeable enough, though she lacked his wife's beauty. Now everywhere there was singing and dancing as the wedding was prepared.

It was at this time that the Frog was making her way to the King's palace. The Frog was indeed a slow traveller! It took her a year and four days to climb the six thousand steps from the Lion-Witch's realm. Then it took another year to prepare to meet the King. She wanted to arrive in style so he would be sure to receive her.

The Frog had a sedan chair made for her and mounted on the back of snail. It was about the size of two eggs and the outside was inlaid with tortoise-shell and the inside lined with lizards' skins.

Fifty frogs from a meadow were chosen as her maids of honour. They too were to ride on snails with finely wrought saddles designed so they could ride side-saddle like fashionable ladies of the time. Next she selected her bodyguards, a vast number of rats whom she had dressed as pages.

For herself, the Frog couldn't resist adding a touch of rouge to her cheeks to match her cap of roses which bloomed as sweetly as ever.

As the Frog and her extraordinary retinue slowly made their way to the palace, sightseers flocked from far and wide. The King and his Bride-To-Be got to hear of it. Their curiosity was aroused, and the Frog had no need to ask for audience: they invited her into the palace.

'I come with news, Oh King,' said the Frog. 'News that will bring you both joy and sorrow. But first, I observe you're unfaithful to your wife and intend to marry again.'

At the mention of his wife, the King began to weep. 'My wife is dead. But her memory is as bright in my heart as ever. But monarchs can't always do as they please, and my subjects insisted that I should marry again. I chose this princess who, as you see, is an admirable young woman.'

'I warn you not to marry her. Your wife is alive and you also have a daughter. But the bad news must follow.' The Frog told him how they were prisoners of the Lion-Witch and gave him the Queen's letter.

The King kissed it and wept and wept and asked a hundred questions about his wife and his daughter.

The envoys who attended the Bride-to-Be were outraged. 'You pledged to marry our Princess. You can't break your promise on the say-so of a Frog! A mere scum from the marshes.'

'I come from the marshes and can travel in water and over the land but I am no scum!' said the Frog.

She gave a sign and at once the snails and rats and even the lizard skins took on a new life. They grew tall and majestic and handsome with eyes that glittered brightly. Each wore a crown studded with jewels and a mantle of velvet lined with ermine with a long train carried by dwarfs.

The sound of trumpets and drums filled the air with military music. The meadow frogs turned into fairies and began to dance and were so light-footed that a jump took them as high as the ceiling.

Suddenly these frog-fairies transformed into flowers: violets, jasmine, carnations, jonquils and roses – but still they danced, like a flower-bed dancing. The King could scarcely believe this was happening! But there it was, happening before him, before his very eyes.

In wonder he watched as the flowers dissolved into fountains. The leaping water cascaded into a lake that encircled the palace. Boats appeared, so prettily painted that the Bride-To-Be couldn't resist asking her envoys to go sailing with her: it would be an amusing pastime before the wedding.

But no sooner had they embarked than the boats and the lake vanished, and the Frog's retinue took on their animal shape again.

'What has become of my Bride-To-Be?' asked the King.

'The Queen is your wife, and she alone should concern you. If I didn't love her as I do,' said the Frog, 'I'd not interfere. But she deserves better than to be the Lion-Witch's prisoner and so does your daughter. It is up to you, O King, to make haste and rescue them.'

'If I were certain my wife was alive, there's nothing I'd shrink from to see her again.' said the King.

The Frog laughed. 'After the marvels you've witnessed, surely you can believe what I say. Now, this is what you must do: leave your kingdom in the care of those whom you trust and depart without delay. Take this ring. It will enable you to see your wife and also to talk to the Lion-Witch, regardless of the fact that she is the most fearsome creature on earth.'

The King decided he would go alone. 'The Queen is my beloved. It is my quest alone to find her.'

Before he set off, he rewarded the Frog with many fine gifts. 'You will encounter fearsome dangers,' she warned him, 'But you are filled with such longing to be united with your wife, I feel that you will succeed.'

Her words gave the King a spurt of courage and he set off to search for the Queen. He begged the ring to guide him and it led him to the forest near the fortress. He wandered to and fro but he could not find the entrance to the Lion-Witch's cavern. Then, one day, he was resting under a tree when he saw a lioness flash by. On her back was his Queen and a beautiful girl who must surely be his daughter.

The King's heart was ablaze. Though time had passed, his wife attracted him more than ever. 'I'd die a thousand deaths sooner than turn back now. he said. 'O ring with your magic powers, guide me to my Queen!'

The ring guided him down the six thousand steps into the Lion-Witch's desolate realm.

The King didn't know the Lion-Witch had foreseen his coming. It was within her power to predict the exact day and time of his arrival. It was not, however, in her power to prevent it. But she would fight him with all her strength.

But first things first, thought the Lion-Witch.

She built a palace of crystal on the Lake of Quicksilver. There she imprisoned the Queen and the Princess. Then she summoned the monsters.

'If you don't help me to drive out the King, he will take your darling away and you'll lose your beautiful princess forever!' she warned them.

The monsters quickly did as she asked and surrounded the crystal palace. The lighter among them stationed themselves on the surrounding wall, on the roof and doors, while the heaviest stayed in the lake.

But it wasn't to the lake that the King went first. The ring guided him to the Lion-Witch's cave. She was waiting for him in her lioness form and as he approached, she sprang.

The King drew his sword with a speed that took the Lion-Witch unawares. As she raised a paw to fell him, a flash of the sword, and he cut off her paw at the elbow. Yelping, she fell and the King stood over her.

One false move and the Lion-Witch knew the King would kill her. She managed to control her rage and as calmly as she could manage she asked: 'What do you want from me? What is it that you want me to do?'

The King, too, managed to contain his anger: if he killed the Lion-Witch he might never learn where she'd hidden his wife. 'What I want,' he said, 'is to punish you for what you have done to my wife. But for the present, return her to me or I shall strangle you here and now with my bare hands.'

The Lion-Witch pointed to the crystal palace and with the aid of the ring, the King saw his wife and daughter.

He called and they heard him. He was overwhelmed with joy. But dismay soon followed as he realised before he could reach them, he'd have to cross the Lake of Quicksilver and evade the threatening monsters.

While he was trying to work out what to do, the Lion-Witch took her chance and vanished. The King cursed himself. He could have made her help him but now it was too late.

He ran down to the edge of the lake. His heart lifted as the crystal palace floated towards him. He made to jump across to it, but then it moved away with with fearsome speed. Again and again the King circled the lake. Again and again the palace came tantalisingly close, then swiftly receded.

The Queen feared he'd give up and urged him on. 'Love can defeat even the Lion-Witch, my King.'

She held out her hands towards him and so did the Princess. The King's strength was restored and he answered, 'I'll die sooner than leave you in this dismal place.'

The King needed all his patience and strength. Three years went by. Three years of sleeping on the ground on a bed of thistles and thorns. Three years of only bitter wild fruits to eat. And not only that, he had to ward off the attacks of the monsters.

How the Queen had survived so long in such a place was a wonder to him. He'd have broken long since, and many a time, he was tempted to fling himself into the lake. He'd have done it and gladly if it would have made life easier for his Queen and daughter.

One day he was running round the lake as usual in the hope of jumping across to the palace, when he saw a huge and and hideous dragon flying towards him.

'I have an offer to make,' he said.

'What offer is that?' demanded the King.

'There is a tasty morsel I've a fancy to eat. If you swear by your crown, sceptre and kingly robe, if you swear also by your wife and your daughter to give it to me at the time I ask, in return,' said the Dragon, 'I will take you to the crystal palace and carry your wife and daughter to safety.'

The King didn't hesitate. 'I swear to you and all your kin you shall have the tasty morsel you desire and I shall be your loyal servant!'

The Dragon warned him if he broke his word, a lifetime's misery would bear down and crush him. But the King's one thought was to rescue his Queen and he repeated his promise.

'Climb on to my back,' said the Dragon.

They flew over the lake to the crystal palace. At once the monsters attacked and the lake belched clouds of sulphur and brimstone.

How savagely the Dragon fought with tooth and claw and fiery breath, and the King fought fiercely at his side. Nor did the Queen merely stand by. She kicked down a wall and armed with a piece of glass, she fought as valiantly as they did.

At last the battle was over. The King and Queen embraced each other and, as they did so, a thunderbolt burst from the sky, plunged into the lake and dried it up. The monsters vanished and so did the Dragon.

What happened then was extraordinary. The King, the Queen and the Princess suddenly found themselves in the dining hall of the royal palace, seated at a richly laden table.

'We are home,' said the King.

It was a moment of pure joy, and he had no premonition of what was soon to come.

THE PRINCESS

The magical appearance of the King, the Queen and the Princess filled the Court and the people with wonder. Above all they marvelled at the Princess, at her beauty, her magnificent gown and the jewels that sparkled so brightly they dazzled the eye.

The Princess herself was astonished when her rags vanished and suddenly she was dressed in such splendour. She was amazed too by the comforts of the palace and rejoiced that now every day she could watch the sun rise and by night see the moon and the stars.

Word of her beauty and wisdom quickly spread and soon princes were arriving from here, there and everywhere, wanting to marry her. Tournaments were held and the princes gave dazzling displays of their skills in the military arts, hoping to impress her. They sang songs in praise of her beauty and wrote poems in her honour.

But the Princess had learnt in the Realm of the Lion-Witch that the fruits which looked most tempting to eat were the most poisonous. She had learnt to look beneath the surface of things with a discerning inner eye. Now she could tell at a glance those princes who were foolish, greedy or vain.

'Choose the husband who pleases you most,' said the King. 'My only wish is that you should be happy.'

Among her suitors was Prince Moufy. He was handsome and the most adept with a sword. Not only that, the Princess saw that he truly loved her. She loved him in return and chose him for her husband.

The Prince had to return to his kingdom to prepare for the wedding, but the Princess begged him to stay. 'I have a such a foreboding that if you go I'll never see you again.'

He was so reluctant to leave her that the Queen gave him a portrait of her daughter and told him to make the wedding preparations simple so he could return without delay. The Prince was glad to agree.

Reassured that he would soon be back, the Princess decided to pass the time learning a musical instrument. She was so eager to learn that soon she surpassed her teacher!

One day the Princess was in her mother's apartment when a Giant arrived on the palace doorstep, asking to see the King.

'I have a message from my master, Mr King, Sir,' he said.

'Who is your master? State your business and be gone,' said the King.

'There's no need to be like that, Mr King, Sir! My master is the Dragon, him who 'as saved your Queen and daughter.'

The King held out his hand. 'Then you are welcome. What can I do for you?'

'My master wants that tasty morsel you promised him,' said the Giant.'

'Whatever he wants, he shall have it and gladly.'

'It's a sweet little morsel he wants, Mr King, Sir. The sweetest in all the world, if you get my drift,' said the Giant.

The King looked puzzled. 'I'm afraid I don't.'

'Why, what else should it be but the Princess, your daughter! There's none sweeter than she and my master has a mind to make her into a pie and eat her for his dinner.'

The King was ashen-faced with horror, as he told the Queen and the Princess what the Dragon demanded.

The Queen gave a scream that pierced his heart and she held her daughter to her. 'I'll die before you give my child to the Dragon. Let him take the kingdom, the crown, the jewels and coins in the treasury – all that we have rather than that!'

'But I gave my word,' wept the King. 'When a king gives his word, he cannot break it.'

The Queen was ablaze with rage. 'What sort of father are you? You'd turn your daughter into a pie sooner than break faith with a dragon! Send the Giant to me. I pray my anguish will soften his heart.'

She turned to the Giant. 'Take all I have,' cried the Queen. 'But spare my daughter.'

'It's not for me to decide,' said the Giant. 'The fact is my master has a singular appetite and when there's someone he's taken a fancy to eat there's nothing in heaven or earth shall alter it. And by way of a warning, Mrs Queen, Ma'am, it's best to give him what he wants when it comes to his dinner, or else it'll be the worse for you and Mr King and the kingdom.'

The Queen fell to the floor in a faint. The Princess was almost fainting too, but she went to tend to her mother.

Three days passed, but the King could not bring himself to hand over daughter. The Giant grew impatient and began to assault them with terrible threats. But the King and Queen agreed that the worst that the Dragon could do was to kill them. 'And if he makes our daughter into a pie, our lives are over anyway!'

Soon after, however, the Giant had a message from the Dragon.

'I tell no word of a lie, I am confounded,' said the Giant. 'Never before has my master forfeited a tasty morsel. But what he says is this.

Instead of making your daughter into a pie, he'll spare her life if she marries his nephew who as it happens is a Prince. And not only is he a Prince, but he's young and handsome. Him and your daughter can be wed and live happily ever after.'

At this, the King and Queen felt a little less grieved and they passed the message on their daughter.

But the Princess had grown up in the harsh realm of the Lion-Witch. Her heart was still loving but, in enduring such hardship, her spirit had grown strong and she'd developed a mind and a will of her own.

'Prince Moufy is my heart's true love. I promised to marry him and I do not chose to go back on that now, for the sake of saving my life. I shall do as the Dragon requests,' said the Princess. 'Then you, my dear parents, will be safe and so will the kingdom.'

The King implored her to change her mind. 'My own, my precious, beloved daughter, don't sacrifice your life to save us.'

The Queen was distraught and again it fell to the Princess to comfort her. But she would not alter her decision and at last her parents were compelled to accept it.

'Not before time,' said the Giant. 'My motto is, "What can't be prevented is best accepted." Now the Princess must go to the mountain-top and my master shall come and fetch her.'

The King and Queen commanded that every honour should attend their daughter. The ancient Ritual of Sacrifice was carried out in every detail.

Four hundred maidens escorted the Princess. They were all of the noblest birth, and they wore long white robes and crowns of cypress. The Princess wore a crown of jasmine and marigolds. Her hair hung over her shoulders, tied with crepe. She was carried aloft in a litter lined with black velvet. The litter was open so that everyone should bear witness to her beauty. The King and Queen walked behind their daughter. The Giant strode in front, heavily armed from head to foot.

Mourners all dressed in black, pale and grey-faced, lined the street. Sobs and cries filled the air but the Princess seemed unmoved by her fate.

The only emotion she showed was at her mother's anguished weeping.

Now they reached the mountain-top. The Giant ordered everyone to make the farewells and depart. They did as they were commanded and went to a nearby hilltop from which they could see the Princess. She stood alone, still, as if frozen. Nor did she flinch when the Dragon came lumbering across the sky.

What a monstrous sight sight he was! His body was covered with huge blue scales and poisonous tongues of fire. His lashing tail had fifty coils and half a coil beyond. Claws as big as windmills tore at the air and his gaping jaws revealed three rows of teeth as long as elephants' tusks. He'd grown so enormous that his six wings would scarcely support him and his progress was slow.

The Queen watched in horror as the Dragon approached her daughter. If only the Frog had let her die in the Realm of the Lion-Witch, she'd have been spared the agony of seeing her daughter devoured. 'Dear Friend,' she cried, 'why did you save me then to desert me now!'

But the Frog had not deserted the Queen. She was speeding on the back of a hawk to tell Prince Moufy what was happening.

She found him mooning over the Princess's portrait. 'That'll do you no good, nor the Princess. She is in dire peril,' she cried. 'You must save her and I shall help you.'

She blew on a leaf from her cap of roses. As her breath touched it, it become a mighty green steed with twelve hoofs and three heads that spat fire and bombshells and cannon balls.

Next she gave him a sword that was eight foot long but as light as a feather. It had a magic sheath to allow him to carry it safely.

'Now put this on,' said the Frog.

It was a coat made out of a single diamond, as hard as rock but so supple it fitted him like a glove and in no way impeded his movements.

The Prince mounted the horse and the Frog told him it would take him to the Princess. 'Do not forget,' she added, 'to tell her the part I have paid in her rescue.'

'Indeed I shall, Ma'am,' said Moufy, 'I am your faithful servant for ever!'

The horse's twelve hooves pounded over the land and the Prince reached the mountain-top at the same time as the Dragon. At once the horse attacked! A volley of cannon balls, bombshells and fire spewed out of its mouths. Twenty cannon balls lodged in the Dragon's throat, his scaly armour was dented and a bombshell put out one eye.

The Dragon howled and flung himself at the Prince with his huge claws bared. But they merely scratched the diamond coat and quick as a lightning flash, the Prince struck back with his sword.

It would be a fight to the death, and they both knew it. The Princess, who'd shown no fear for herself, was now trembling with fear for her Prince as she saw the Dragon charge again. He threw the Prince to the ground, but the Prince leapt back up on to his horse. Again he was thrown. Again he leapt up. Five times in all.

Now in a frenzy of pain and rage, the Dragon went in for the kill. On they fought, on and on. Claws, teeth and wings littered the ground and the earth was wet with blood, the mingled green blood of the Prince's horse and the red blood of the Dragon.

It was the Dragon who wearied first. He fell to the ground, and the Prince struck the fatal blow. Extraordinarily, no blood flowed.

Out of the gaping wound stepped a Prince, young, handsome, elegantly dressed in a coat of blue and gold velvet embroidered with pearls. On his head was a small helmet with a crest of white feathers. He ran towards the astounded Prince Moufy and embraced him.

'How can I ever repay you!' he cried. 'You've delivered me from the Lion-Witch's curse. For sixteen years, she imprisoned me in a dragon's skin, the worst prison a man can know. It was she who commanded me to devour the Princess, and such was her power I could only obey.'

'We must offer a prayer of thanks to the Unseen Power who has saved us both,' said the Princess.

Then the Prince told her how the Frog had warned him of her danger.

'Look!' said the Queen.

Through the sky came a hawk with golden bells on its feet that tinkled as it flew. On its back was the Frog herself with her cap of roses blooming as sweetly as ever.

The Queen ran joyfully to greet her and, as she took the little paw the Frog held out to her, the Frog transformed into a Queen with a majestic gracious presence. Silence fell as the Frog began to speak:

'I have come to crown the Princess who chose to face death rather than to betray her heart. Also, to crown the Prince who is as valiant and true as she.'

She crowned the lovers with crowns of myrtles. Then she tapped the dragon's bones three times with her wand. The bones rose up and formed themselves into a triumphal arch to celebrate the blessed occasion.

The Princess and the Prince led the way back to the city. They were married the next day and the people rejoiced throughout the land.

PUSS IN BOOTS

In a time when the rich were very rich and the poor were very poor, a miller lived in a small kingdom. He was so poor that, when he died, all he had to leave his three sons were his mill, his ass and his cat. For reasons best known to himself he left the mill to his eldest son, his ass to the second son and the Cat to the youngest son, whose name was William.

William felt very hard done by. His two brothers could get together with the mill and the ass and make a living, but what could he do with a cat? 'I could make a muff out of his skin, I suppose,' he muttered. 'But what's the point? After that, I'd be left with nothing!'

He sat by the roadside and moaned and moaned. The Cat pretended to be asleep but in fact, he was all ears and listening. At last he could stand it no longer.

'If I might be allowed to get a word in, young Master.'

'Go ahead. I've nothing else to do! I may as well listen to you as do anything.'

'To begin with, let's have no more complaints about your inheritance, that all that your father left you was me!'

'Oh dear, I'm sorry Cat. It's just that I….'

'Don't start up again. Listen, young Master.'

William fell silent and listened.

'What I shall achieve for you, are riches such as you never dreamed of. But you'll have to trust me,' said the Cat, 'and do as I say without "Whys?" and "Wherefores?" Understood?'

His young Master knew the Cat was clever and cunning. He'd often admired the tricks he played to catch the mice in his father's barn: he would hide in the flour or hang from the rafters, then suddenly pounce and make his kill.

But making him rich was a different matter! William couldn't imagine how the Cat could do that, 'But I suppose I've nothing to lose. What do you want me to do?'

'I want you to fetch me a leather bag, young Master.'

'A leather bag!' wailed William. 'You might as well ask for the sun and the moon! I don't own one and I can't buy one. I'm the youngest son and I haven't a penny.'

William seemed set to wail on forever! But then he remembered his jacket was leather. 'If you must have a bag, very well, I'll make one.'

Soon the bag was finished. But the Cat had another demand. He wanted a pair of leather boots so he could walk without feeling the pricking of thorns or the sharp edges of stones. 'And I want them made to fit, young Master, so they neither pinch nor squeeze.'

William started wailing again, 'Leather boots indeed! You might as well ask for the sun and moon! I'm the youngest son and I haven't a penny.'

The Cat was losing patience. He might have stalked off but just in time William had an idea. His own boots were worn but they were made of leather. If he re-cut them, they'd make a pair of boots for the Cat. 'I'll have to go barefoot. But I've nowhere to go, so what does it matter!'

He set to work and didn't stop till the boots were finished.

'An excellent fit, young Master. Now I'll be off,' said the Cat.

William asked where he was going but the Cat wouldn't answer. 'I said, "No questions". And try to cheer up. All will be well. Wait here till I return.'

In his new leather boots with the leather bag slung round his neck, the Cat hurried off down the road. He knew just where he was going!

First he went to the barn. Some bran had fallen to the floor. He scooped it up and put it into the bag. Next he picked a clump of wild lettuces which were growing by the roadside. These too he put into the bag. Then he headed for a field with a large rabbit warren.

There were no rabbits in sight, they were all at home in the safety of the warren. But he laid the bag on the ground and stretched out beside it, as still as a branch on a windless day.

Soon a young rabbit came out of the warren. He thought the Cat was dead, that he'd nothing to fear. Looking forward to a meal of bran and lettuce, he hoped into the bag, hoppity hop!

Very much alive the Cat sprang to his feet. 'You've fallen into my trap, young fellow. You could have checked I was dead, but you didn't.'

The Cat showed neither pity nor mercy. He fastened the bag and killed the rabbit. Then he went on his way to the royal palace.

Boldly he demanded to see the King. He was taken to a large room hung with silk and thickly carpeted, where the King sat on his throne. 'Your Majesty, I bring a gift from my master's rabbit warren. He would be honoured if you would accept it.'

'Who is your master?' enquired the King.

The Cat bowed with a flourish. 'My master, Your Majesty, is a great lord, Monsieur le Marquis le Carabas.'

'I don't know the name,' said the King.

The Cat made no answer to this! He'd made up the name on the spot, thinking the King might refuse a gift from a miller's son called William.

He waited as the King inspected the rabbit.

'It is plump and tender,' he said at last. 'Thank the Marquis for his gift. I shall accept it.'

The Cat hurried back to find his young Master sitting just where he'd left him. He was feeling so sorry for himself he didn't even ask the Cat where he'd been.

'It's all over for me, Cat. If I don't die of cold, then hunger will kill me. Oh if I only I had a mill or an ass like my brothers. If only....'

'Enough! Haven't I told you,' cried the Cat, 'that I'll make you rich beyond your wildest imagining, that soon your brothers will envy you! All is I ask is a little patience!'

At once William apologised. 'You're right, Cat. I'm an ungrateful ninny. And I dare say I'll survive somehow. There are berries in the hedgerows to eat and it's quite pleasant sleeping out at this time of year.'

He managed not to moan again for one full week.

'Now it's time I was off again,' said the Cat.

'How long will you be?'

'As long as it takes.'

The Cat went directly to a wheatfield where partridges were feeding. There was plenty of wheat for them to eat but when the Cat put the bag on the ground and opened it, one partridge, then another, couldn't resist walking in to see if there was something more tasty inside it.

At once the Cat pounced. 'Fools!!' he cried. 'If you don't know when you're on to a good thing, you deserve neither pity nor mercy.'

He fastened the bag and killed the partridges and took them to the King.

'I bring these birds as a gift, Majesty, from my master Monsieur le Marquis le Carabas.'

This time the King didn't hesitate. 'Give my thanks to the Marquis, they are quality birds with plenty of flesh.' Then he gave the Cat a tip, a gold coin, for bringing them to him.

Young William sat glumly by the roadside. But he cheered up at once at the sight of the coin. 'Where have you been? Where did you get it?'

'I said, no questions. But I'll tell you this, young Master. I earned it by using my wits and my cunning.'

For the next few months the Cat continued to go off hunting and to take his kill to the King as gifts from his master, Monsieur le Marquis le Carabas. And the King would reward him with a gold coin so that now, with money in his pocket, William had no need to sleep by the roadside with nothing to eat but wild berries.

'I haven't a mill or an ass like my brothers. But thanks to you, Cat, if I'm not the richest man in the world I'm no longer the poorest.'

'There is more yet to come!' said the Cat.

Soon after they heard that the King was taking his daughter for a ride along the river bank in his carriage. The Princess, everyone knew, was the most beautiful in all the world. But she was very shy and rarely ventured out of the palace.

'I shall stand by the roadside and salute her,' said William.

'No, you won't. You'll jump in the river. Be quick about it,' said the Cat.

'But I can't swim! I'll drown!'

'It's up to you. But in your place, I'd trust someone who'd brought me a gold coin every week for months on end. The river looks deep, but it isn't.'

William looked down into the water. It looked very deep to him! But on the other hand, the prospect of untold riches was tempting, and he had to die one day.

'All right, Cat, I'll do as you say. I'll risk it.'

Without more ado, he stripped and jumped SPLASH! into the river as the carriage passed by.

'Help!' shouted the Cat. 'Monsieur le Marquis le Carabas is drowning!'

The King stopped the carriage and told his guards to go to the aid of the Marquis who'd sent him so many fine gifts.

Even the Princess forget her shyness. 'Hurry,' she urged. 'Hurry.'

Her voice reached William as he sank towards the murky depths. It gave him a spurt of strength and he thrashed and floundered in the water and managed to keep afloat till the guards pulled him out with a pole.

Now his Master was safe, the crafty Cat hid his shabby shirt and shabbier trousers under a stone. 'Alas, alack!' he cried. 'Thieves have stolen the Marquis's clothes.'

'Fetch a suit from my wardrobe!' commanded the King. Again the Princess urged the servants, 'Hurry, Hurry.'

The servants quickly returned with a suit of best silk. The Cat noted with satisfaction it set off his Master's good looks to advantage. He noted, too, that the Princess cast him an admiring glance. As for the King, he was so taken by the young man's handsome appearance that he invited him into the carriage. 'You shall ride with us, Monsieur le Marquis.'

William looked round to see who the King was talking to and realised with astonishment that it was him, that he was the Marquis! Very puzzled, he climbed in. Then the Princess looked up shyly and smiled at him. The smile went straight to his heart: instantly he was in love.

The Cat grinned to himself and ran on to a meadow where peasants were cutting hay. 'Heed me well, my good fellows,' he snarled. 'If you don't tell the King that this meadow belongs to Monsieur le Marquis le Carabas, you'll be chopped into into little pieces, like meat for a pâté. Understood?'

The Cat had such a look about him that the terrified peasants hastened to assure him they'd do as he said.

A few minutes later the carriage came by and the King paused to admire the crop. 'To whom does this meadow belong?' he asked.

The peasants were quick to reply, 'It belongs to Monsieur le Marquis le Carabas, Sire.'

The King turned to William. 'You have a valuable asset in this meadow.'

William paused for just a moment. If the King said he was a Marquis and the peasants said the meadow was his, he wasn't going to argue. 'Indeed, Your Majesty, the meadow gives a good crop every year,' he answered.

On ran the Cat to a field where the men were harvesting the wheat. 'Heed me well, my good fellows,' he snarled. 'If you don't tell the King that this field belongs to Monsieur le Marquis le Carabas, you'll be chopped into little pieces, like meat for a pâté. Understood?'

Like the mowers before them, the harvesters didn't feel inclined to argue. When the King passed by and asked, 'Whose wheatfield is this with its splendid crop?', they were quick to reply that it belonged to Monsieur le Marquis le Carabas.

And so it went on. The Cat kept running on ahead of the carriage and threatening the peasants and workers with a terrible fate if they did not say the crops they were harvesting belonged to Monsieur le Marquis le Carabas.

Then he waited for the carriage to catch up to listen to what William and the King were saying.

'You're a young man of vast wealth, Monsieur le Marquis,' said the King.

'I have my father to thank, Majesty, for the inheritance he left me.' answered William.

The carriage window was open and the Cat smiled as he heard his young Master's reply. Only he fully understood its meaning! As for the King and the Princess, they were now as much impressed by the way the Marquis honoured his father as by his riches.

At full speed, the Cat raced on until he came to a castle. Not an ordinary castle, but a huge castle of great magnificence that belonged to an Ogre, and that Ogre owned all the lands which the Cat had claimed for his master.

It's win all, lose all, thought the Cat. He'd reached the last stage of his plan, and the most dangerous. He crossed the drawbridge and knocked on the door. There was the Ogre, towering before him. 'What do you want? What brings you to my castle?'

'I couldn't pass by without paying respects to the biggest ogre in the world,' said the Cat.

The Ogre was flattered and invited him inside.

'I've been told, Sir, that you have remarkable powers. That you can turn yourself into whatsoever you please.'

'And so I can!' roared the Ogre. 'And to prove it, I'll turn myself into a lion!'

As the huge beast snapped and snarled before him, the Cat jumped from the window up on to the guttering. His boots weren't made for walking on roofs and he slipped and slithered dangerously.

At last the Ogre turned back into himself again.

The Cat clambered down, shivering. 'I know a lion is only a larger version of myself, for what is a lion if not a cat? But I won't deny I've never been so frightened in my life!'

He made a great show of how scared he'd been and nothing could have pleased the Ogre more! He was immensely proud of his power to strike terror in all who encountered him.

'To turn yourself into a lion is a remarkable feat,' said the Cat. 'But I've heard you can do something even more extraordinary.'

"I dare say I can. What is it?' asked the Ogre.

'That you, the largest Ogre in the world, can turn yourself into the smallest of creatures, a rat or a mouse for example. Of course, it's only what I've heard. For myself, I can't believe it.'

'Can't you believe it indeed! Then watch this!'

At once the Ogre became a mouse! The Cat seized his chance. He pounced on the Ogre-Mouse. Without pity or mercy, he killed it and ate it.

At that very moment, the King's carriage was crossing the drawbridge; he'd seen the castle in the distance and wanted to take a closer look.

The Cat hurried out to greet him. 'Welcome, Majesty, to the castle of my master, Monsieur le Marquis le Carabas.'

The King had never seen a better built castle with so many outbuildings and courtyards. 'Is this all yours too, Monsieur le Marquis! I'd like to look round, I'm very impressed.'

William gazed at the castle. Can this truly be mine? he wondered. But the Cat had said so and the fact was, he was the Cat's master and he knew the Cat would never deceive him. All this is mine, he thought, and what's more, I am now a Marquis. The Marquis offered his hand to the Princess and followed the King through the mighty doorway.

A meal was laid out in the banqueting hall. The Ogre had been expecting guests, other monsters like himself, but the Cat knew they wouldn't dare come now that the King was present.

'Your Majesty,' said the Cat, 'Monsieur le Marquis le Carabas would be honoured if you and the Princess would dine with him.'

The Princess and the Marquis picked at their food, and feasted their eyes on each other! But the King ate heartily and, after six glasses of wine, he began to think that the Marquis would make a fine husband for his daughter. He was handsome and rich and seemed a good natured fellow.

'If you wish to marry the Princess, I'd have no objection,' he said.

The young couple were so besotted with each other that they begged that a priest be summoned at once, and they were married there and then.

The Cat noted that his master took to his new life as if he'd been born to it. Indeed, as the days passed, the Marquis seemed to lose all memory of himself as William, the poor miller's son.

I wonder if he remembers whom he has to thank for his good fortune! thought the Cat.

He lay down on the floor as if he were dead, a trick he had used in the past. He was sure that the Marquis would weep and grieve and, at the very least, order a gold coffin to be made for him.

When the Marquis came into the room and found the Cat lying still and stiff, he sent at once for a servant.

'Get this corpse out of here!' he commanded. 'Do with it what you please, but get rid of it!'

The Cat sprang to his feet with a howl of indignation. 'What kind of gratitude is that,' he raged.

He wasn't staying where he wasn't valued. He jumped from the window and headed off and away beyond the castle grounds. He was never heard of again.

And Monsieur le Marquis le Carabas? As far as is known, he didn't suffer from the Cat's departure and lived happily ever after.

RED RIDING HOOD

This is a story with two endings and one beginning. It begins like this: On the edge of a forest was a wood and on the edge of the wood was a village. In this village all the girls were pretty. But the prettiest by far was called Biddy.

Biddy's Ma adored her pretty daughter. Biddy was the joy of her life in fact! She loved the way her hair curled, the light in her eyes and the heart-shaped dimple under her chin.

As for Biddy, she thought her Ma was the sweetest ever!

She didn't plague her with do's and don'ts.

She never fussed or scolded, let alone beat her!

Not even when she went to the Vagabonds Fair until well after tea-time!

'You are lucky, Biddy,' the other girls sighed.

They loved their mothers, but they couldn't help wishing they were more like Biddy's and would let them do whatever they pleased!

It wasn't just her Ma who doted on Biddy. Her little old Gran had only to look at her and her heart would warm and glow with delight. She called her pet names like 'Sweet Darling' or 'Gran's Little Princess' and she was for ever making the sugar iced cakes which Biddy was so fond of.

When Biddy's birthday came, her little old Gran would spend days on end trying to think of something special to give her. One year she was completely stumped for an idea. As always she would give Biddy something to wear, something to show Biddy off for the Little Beauty she was – but what?

A clasp for her hair? A necklace? A dress? But Biddy's wardrobe was bursting with dresses and she had a box filled to the brim with trinkets.

'I know what!' cried Gran. 'For my Sweet Treasure's birthday I'll make her a cloak!'

She was was so excited that, without even thinking to change out of her slippers, she ran through the forest, through the wood, and on to the village to tell Biddy's Ma what she'd decided.

Biddy's Ma was ecstatic. 'Our Pretty Pet is just of an age to be wanting a cloak.'

'It will be no common cloak either!' said Gran. 'But a cloak of the best velvet, lined with silk, with a hood trimmed about with fur!'

'What colour shall you make it?'

'The colour that's right for her.'

'How about blue?' Biddy's Ma said.

'Blue might do for the sea and sky. But not for our Biddy,' said Gran.

'Then how about green?'

'Green might do for the grass in the fields. But not our Biddy.'

'Well, what about yellow?'

'Yellow might do for the sun or even the moon! But no, it's not right for our Biddy.'

Then together, with one voice, they both said: 'Red is the colour that's right for our Biddy.'

'It'll match the apples in her cheeks,' said her Ma.

'It will set off her chestnut brown hair,' said Gran.

She hurried home and set to work. Day after day, night after night, she stitched and stitched until her eyes ached and her fingers grew weary. But the cloak was ready in time for Biddy's birthday.

Her Ma and her Gran couldn't wait to see how she looked in it. They slipped the soft velvet around her shoulders and tied the long flowing ribbons of the hood into a bow under her chin.

Biddy spun around in a circle so the cloak swung about her. 'It's the darlingest cloak, Gran! I just love it!'

She ran off down the street to show her friends. Her Gran and her Ma noted with pride that every head turned to admire her!

'Pretty as a picture, she is!' said her Ma.

'Pretty as a princess,' said Gran.

From that time on Biddy wore the cloak wherever she went. Soon she was no longer called Biddy. Everyone called her Red Riding Hood.

One morning Red Riding Hood came into the kitchen to find her Ma all fussed and flummoxed. She'd had word that Gran had taken to her bed because she was poorly, and she was too busy to visit her.

'I'm up to my eyes this morning,' she said. 'But I've baked her some scones and made a pot of fresh butter. Would you take them for me, my Pretty Precious?'

'Yes, of course, darling Ma. You know how I love my dear little Gran,' said Red Riding Hood.

Her Ma had packed the scones and butter into a basket and Red Riding Hood set off without delay.

She hadn't gone far when she met some of her friends making daisy chains in a meadow.

'Where are you going, Red Riding Hood?' they called.

'I'm going through the wood, through the forest to visit my Gran. She's poorly, you see, and I'm taking her scones and fresh butter which Ma has sent for her.'

The other girls wished that they could go with her. But they didn't dare!

'My mother says I mustn't go to the forest.'

'My mother says I mustn't go to the wood.'

'If I take one step beyond this meadow she'll skin me alive, my mother says!'

Red Riding Hood was horrified. 'How perfectly awful! Well my Ma doesn't mind in the least. In fact it's my Ma who's sent me.'

So saying, she went on her way into the wood.

It was a sunny day. The sky was clear and the only clouds to be seen were soft fluffy white ones that drifted lazily in the breeze. A feeling of happiness filled Red Riding Hood as she skipped down the path that led through the wood and on into the forest.

Here the trees grew tall. Red Riding Hood paused and gazed admiringly up at the long slender trunks that stretched high above and their branches spread wide.

Just then a Wolf came by. He might have missed her, she was standing so still. But her cloak caught his eye and he crept quietly up to see what was inside.

When he saw Red Riding Hood his nose twitched. 'She's young and juicy and tender! She'll go down a treat for my dinner!'

He was just about to pounce. But then the sound of axes came ringing through the forest. Axes meant men. And men meant danger. If he tried to eat her there and then, he was afraid that her screams would bring them running.

A younger wolf might have risked it, but he was an old wolf and a very wily one. He'd have the little girl for his dinner! But he'd plot and plan and bide his time.

He put on a smile, raised his hat and bowed with a flourish.

'Good day to you, my Pretty.'

When she saw the Wolf standing before her, Red Riding Hood could have turned and fled. She could have called the woodcutters to come to her to her aid. She could have done both.

But she did neither! She'd never heard that wolves could be dangerous! That it was better by far not to stop to find out! Her Ma hadn't told her, nor had her Gran. Perhaps they'd forgotten or didn't know, for no Gran or Ma in the world can know everything!

Poor little Red Riding Hood – she never guessed for one minute that this tall handsome wolf with his beautiful manners and elegant clothes intended to eat her!

She dimpled sweetly and flashed him a smile. 'Good day, Mr Wolf.'

'That's a very pretty cloak! And such a pretty hood, all trimmed with fur.'

'Indeed it is, Mr Wolf. I wear it everywhere and everyone calls me Red Riding Hood.'

Again the Wolf bowed. 'Your servant, Red Riding Hood. If I might be so bold, where are you going alone through the forest?'

'I'm going to visit my dear little Gran. She's poorly, you see, and I'm taking some scones and fresh butter which Ma has sent for her.'

'Where does she live, your dear little Gran?'

'She lives where the forest dips into the valley. It's the first house you come to. No one could miss it.'

When he heard this, the Wolf's eyes glinted. If he planned it right, he'd have not just the little girl but also her Gran for his dinner.

'I'd like to meet your little old Gran.'

'She's truly a dear. I'm sure that you'll like her.'

'I'm sure that I shall. Now, I'll take this path and you take the other. We'll make a game of it and see who gets to your little Gran's first!'

'Oh yes, what fun!' Red Riding Hood cried.

'One, two, three and off we go!'

The Wolf had chosen the shortest path for himself and off he ran at full speed though the forest.

The path he'd chosen for Little Red Riding Hood took the long way round, winding this way and that. It took her past trees heavy with nuts, and clearings brilliant with flowers and brightly coloured butterflies.

She couldn't resist stopping to gather the nuts. And the flowers were so pretty that she simply had to pick some. And then what fun to run with the butterflies here and there, hither and thither.

She forget about her Gran and the game with the Wolf and, by the time she remembered, the Wolf was already knocking on Gran's door.

So as not to alert the old lady that danger threatened, the cunning creature knocked softly, just as a girl might. TAPPITY TAP!

'Who's there?' called Gran.

Now the Wolf made his voice sweet and clear. 'It's Red Riding Hood, Gran. I've bought you scones and fresh butter which Ma has sent for you.'

'Bless you, dear. I'm in bed, but you can let yourself in. Pull out the peg and lift the latch.'

The Wolf pulled out the peg and lifted the latch. He opened the door and walked straight in. Without more ado, he gobbled up Gran!

He gobbled her whole, every bit of her! Her nightgown, her nightcap and even her shawl!

The Wolf wiped his whiskers. 'I've had my starter! Now to wait for the rest of my dinner.'

Soon after, never guessing what was in store for her, Red Riding Hood skipped up the path and knocked on the door. TAPPITY TAP!

'Who's there?' called the Wolf.

In his greedy excitement, his voice came out in a deep gruff growl.

Red Riding Hood paused with a puzzled frown. 'That doesn't sound like my little old Gran. But who else could it be! She must have a cold and it's made her voice hoarse.'

'It's me, Gran,' she called, 'your darling Red Riding Hood.'

This time the Wolf made his voice tender like little old Gran's. 'Pull out the peg, dear, and then lift the latch.'

Red Riding Hood pulled the peg and lifted the latch. She opened the door and walked straight in.

Quickly the Wolf dived under the quilt. It covered him up from head to toe. All Red Riding saw a lump in the bed!

'Good day to you, Gran. I've brought scones and fresh butter which Ma has sent for you.'

The wicked Wolf grinned under the quilt. He had had something else in mind for dinner!

'Put the scones in the breadbin, my little Morsel!'

'Yes, Gran.'

'Put the butter in the pantry, my Tasty Dear.'

'Yes, Gran.'

'Now my Sweetling, make yourself warm and get in beside me.'

Red Riding Hood climbed up into the bed. She'd never seen her Gran without her clothes on and was greatly surprised by what she saw.

'Why Gran, what big arms you've got!'

The Wolf thought fast and quickly came back with the answer: 'All the better to hug you with, my little Pet!'

'And what big legs you've got!'

'All the better to run with, my dear little Angel!'

'And what big ears you've got!' gasped Red Riding Hood.

'All the better to hear you with, my own sweet Precious!'

'And what big eyes you've got!'

'All the better to see you with, my tender darling!'

'And what big, big teeth!'

The Wolf opened his big mouth wide: 'All the better to eat you with!'

That was that! He gobbled her whole, just as he'd gobbled her Gran.

And some will say that was the end of Gran and Riding Hood....

And some will say that what happened was this: the wolf fell asleep after his big meal. He slept with his mouth open and his loud snores filled the house and floated out through the windows and up the chimney.

A Woodcutter, passing by on his way home from work, was very surprised to hear such immensely loud snores coming from Gran's house! Gran was a little woman and, even if she tried, she couldn't have snored as loudly as that. But it's none of my business, he thought.

He was about to go on his way when another snore reached him, a snore so deep it was almost a grunt. The Woodcutter felt his hackles rise. He knew there were wolves in the forest. It would do no harm to check that all was well with little old Gran. He knocked on the door. RAP! RAP! RATATAT!

There was no reply but the Woodcutter knew there was someone inside. 'I can hear snores. And if it's not Gran, I mean to know who it is!'

He pulled out the peg, lifted the latch, opened the door and walked straight in. There on the bed he saw the Wolf sound asleep, with a fat bulging belly.

The Woodcutter guessed at once what had happened. 'He's gone and eaten Gran for his dinner!'

Quick as a flash, with one blow of his axe, he killed the sleeping Wolf. Then he picked up a knife from the table and cut him wide open.

To the Woodcutter's amazement, out climbed not just Gran but also Red Riding Hood. She looked about her, confused and bewildered: 'It was ever so dark in there!'

'Indeed it was!' said her little old Gran.

'It was lucky I was passing. You'd not have lasted in there much longer! And now, before I go,' the Woodcutter said, 'there's one more thing that I must do.'

He fetched his knife and skinned the Wolf. Then he nailed the skin to a tree as a warning to any other wolf in the forest who might be thinking of eating a little old Gran or a little girl for his dinner.

So, did Red Riding Hood and her Gran end up in the Wolf? Or did the Wolf end up with his skin nailed to the tree? I can't make up my mind which ending is true. So I'll leave it to you to decide....

RIQUET THE TUFT

There once was a time when fairies took more interest in the lives of humans than nowadays. Some gave great and wonderful gifts to a newborn child; others were not so kind, and gave curses and misfortune to the unlucky victim.

The Fairy in this particular story did neither exactly the one nor exactly the other. She had her own way of doing things where humans were concerned. When a child was born, she might grant the baby some wonderful gift. But then she would match it with a dreadful affliction in the same measure.

This is what happened when one Queen gave birth to a son: the Fairy cursed the boy with such ugliness that his mother screamed when she saw him. 'Oh the poor mite!' she cried. 'Was there ever such a hideous child?'

She begged the Fairy to give him one good feature. 'Could you give him a pair of straight eyes instead of a squint? Or a straight back instead of a hump? Or at least a nose that doesn't look like a beetroot? Or make him tall instead of small and scrawny?'

But the Fairy replied that she couldn't alter what she had done. 'However,' she said, 'your son shall not be without his assets. He shall be as clever as he is ugly.'

'I suppose that's something,' said his mother.

But the Fairy hadn't finished. 'I will give also him the power to make the woman he loves best as intelligent as himself.'

With this, the Fairy vanished.

As the years passed, the Queen waited hopefully for her son to grow a little less ugly. But alas, he didn't. In fact, he developed another unsightly feature: a tuft of hair that stuck up on the top of his head. Soon everyone called him Riquet the Tuft.

He was extraordinarily ugly. But he was also quite astoundingly clever. From his crib, little Riquet would offer the soundest advice to men many times his years on matters of business and science and politics. He could do complex sums in his head and learn a new language in a week.

Soon after Riquet was born, the Queen in the kingdom next door had two daughters. On both occasions the Fairy was present. She blessed the first child with exceptional beauty. The proud mother was in raptures. 'What a little beauty she is!' she cried. She babbled on and on about her daughter's good looks!

Maybe it was this that caused the Fairy to say, 'Beauty your daughter has. But brains she shall lack. She shall be the most beautiful princess in the world, and the most stupid.'

The Queen was dismayed. 'But beauty without brains is like butter with no bread to put it on,' she complained.

'What is given is given,' said the Fairy. 'But I shall also give her the power to make the man she loves as beautiful as she is.'

Soon after, the Queen had another daughter. Once more the Fairy was in attendance and the Queen fervently hoped she would bless her second child with the beauty of the first and perhaps brains as well! But like Riquet's mother before her, she had to bite back a scream when she saw the new-born baby.

'What an ugly little thing!' she cried, 'Oh, the unfortunate darling!'

'She may be ugly but she shall have all the brains her sister lacks, and more,' said the Fairy.

With that, the Queen had to be satisfied. She had a daughter who was beautiful and stupid, and another who was clever and ugly. But the Fairy had spoken and there was nothing to be done but accept it.

To the Queen's relief, however, the Princesses didn't squabble like some sisters and each admired in the other the gift that she lacked.

It was the eldest Princess, however, who felt she was by far the less fortunate. Being beautiful was all very well. But after people had looked at you for five minutes and praised your eyes and your hair and the curve of your lips – what then? If you couldn't remember their names or even your own, if you hardly knew whether the sun came out by night or by day, they soon got bored. Off they went to talk to her sister who mightn't be much to look at it, but whose conversation sparkled with wit.

The Princess was as clumsy as she was stupid. She couldn't walk across the room without tripping over her feet or drink her soup without going off in a dream so she spilt it down her dress. Even her mother became exasperated with her.

'Was there ever such a stupid girl?' she sighed.

The Princess agreed that there wasn't and when people shunned her, she didn't blame them. She became so unhappy that one day she took herself off, all alone, to the wood that divided the two kingdoms.

She hadn't walked far when she came face to face with the ugliest man she had ever seen. He was richly dressed, however, and she managed to work out that he must be a prince. And so indeed he was! It was Riquet the Tuft himself.

Riquet couldn't believe his good fortune! He had never met the Princess, but he'd seen her portrait and he was already madly in love with her.

He introduced himself and paid her one compliment after another. He praised the gold in her hair, the deep blue of her eyes, the grace of her walk and so on. The Princess had heard it all a hundred times before and she grew more and more depressed.

Riquet exercised all his brains but he still couldn't work out why a Princess who was blessed with such beauty should suffer a moment's unhappiness. The intelligent thing, he thought, was to ask her, but in a roundabout way so as not to offend her.

'Lovely Lady,' he began, 'I've seen many many beautiful women in my life but never one to match you.'

The Princess rummaged in her mind for an answer. She'd heard of Riquet's awesome cleverness and hoped that if she said as little as possible, she wouldn't reveal what a stupid she was.

'It's good of you to say so,' was all she replied.

'Beauty is such an advantage. If I had a fraction of your beauty,' went on Riquet the Tuft, 'I'm sure I'd be happy forever!'

'Well, I'd give it up tomorrow for all the good it's done me!' The Princess felt so strongly in the matter, she didn't pause to consider what she said next: 'I'd much rather be clever even if it meant being as monstrously ugly as you.'

A cleverer girl might have used more tact! But Riquet the Tuft wasn't offended. 'You may be more intelligent than you think, Princess. Those who believe they lack intelligence usually possess it, and vice versa.'

The Princess frowned. 'That's all too clever for me. All I know is that I'm stupid and so wretched because of it, I wish I could die!'

Riquet the Tuft was greatly alarmed. 'I trust that you'll do no such thing! If your lack of brains is all that distresses you, I can put that right in a trice.'

The Princess looked at him in disbelief. But she summoned all the attention she could muster as he said: 'When I was born, a Fairy gave me the power to give intelligence to the woman I love best. You are that woman. If you will marry me, your intelligence shall equal mine.'

Marry him! The Princess was so stunned that she couldn't reply.

Riquet the Tuft took this to mean she needed time to think it over. 'Of course you will want time to consider. But it's an offer, dear Princess, that should suit us both and I've no doubt that you will accept it,' said Riquet. 'I suggest that we meet here at the same time a year from today. You can give me a definite answer and we can arrange our wedding.'

The Princess tried to gather such brains as she had to work out what to do. She wasn't in the least sure she wanted to marry Riquet, now or ever, he was so hideously ugly. But one thing she was sure of, she wanted intelligence more than anything. But I'm such a stupid, she thought, if I don't give him an answer now, I'll forget Riquet's offer within five minutes. Then I'll remain stupid forever.

'I'll marry you, Riquet,' she said.

No sooner had she spoken than the Princess felt a change come over her. Suddenly her mind was full of the cleverest things to say. She found herself talking with ease about complex affairs of state, the latest scientific inventions and what was happening on the stock exchange.

Riquet the Tuft began to wonder if he'd given the Princess more intelligence than he'd kept for himself! But he still longed to marry her, and couldn't wait to meet her again in a year's time.

'I said I would give you a year and so I shall,' said Riquet. 'Good day to you, my Princess.'

When she returned to the palace, everyone listened in wonder as the Princess began to speak with as much intelligence as she'd babbled before. Even the King invited her into the council chamber for the benefit of her advice. Only her sister was a little put out, finding herself outshone in brains as well as in beauty; but she had too many brains of her own to make a fuss about it.

News of the Princess's transformation spread far and wide. Soon Princes came flocking, all wanting to marry her.

The Princess used her newly-given judgment to see through those who were weak, silly, ignorant or obnoxiously proud. But at last she met a Prince who was not only agreeable but also clever, rich and very handsome. She couldn't help feeling attracted to him.

The King knew of her engagement to Riquet the Tuft. 'But the fact is, my daughter, he is a ugly brute. And where your heart is concerned, you are your own mistress. You shall marry whomsoever you please.'

The Princess was surprised that her father had not insisted that she keep her promise to Riquet. She almost wished he had done! As it was she was left to decide for herself and, contrary to what she had at first expected, her intelligence was less help than hindrance.

One part of her brain said, 'Riquet the Tuft is a truly good man and I can't deny he has touched my heart.'

Another part replied, 'He might be good and honest but he is ugly.'

And yet another spoke up for the Prince. 'He is a perfectly splendid man. Think what a fine couple you will make.'

'But you like Riquet better....'

'But the Prince has fine eyes....'

'I might as well be as stupid as I was before, for all I can make up my mind!' said the Princess.

The months went by and the Princess was as undecided as ever.

One morning, hoping to calm her agitated mind, she went to the wood where she'd met Riquet the Tuft. As she walked, she seemed to hear a muffled noise coming from under the ground. It sounded as if as if a great number of people were bustling about below. Then she heard a voice....

'Bring me the stock pot!' said the voice.

'Give me a copper pan,' called another.

'Put some wood on the fire,' shouted a third.

Suddenly, the earth opened up. There, at her feet, was a cave that contained a huge kitchen with any number of cooks and kitchen hands preparing what promised to be a magnificent feast.

The Princess was yet more astonished when twenty or so cooks emerged from the cave. They were big brawny fellows who seemed to specialise in roasting, for they set up spits and began to roast enormous joints. Each one held a spoon to baste with in one hand, and a fox's tail hung behind one ear. They began to sing.

The Princess was curious. 'Who is your master? Who is the feast for?'

The Head Cook bowed and replied, 'Our master is Riquet the Tuft. The

feast is for his wedding tomorrow to the King's eldest daughter.'

The Princess gasped. Then she remembered; it was exactly a year since she'd promised to return to discuss her marriage with Riquet. Her mind at the time had been as full of holes as a sieve, and the date that the promise fell due had slipped out of it.

Not knowing what else to do, she continued her walk. Then she saw Riquet striding towards her. He looks very pleased with himself, she thought, though he's as ugly as ever.

'Here I am, Princess,' said Riquet. 'Right on time, punctual as always.'

'So I see.'

'I knew you'd be here, waiting for me.'

'Did you, indeed?' said the Princess.

'I never doubted it.'

The Princess raised an eyebrow, 'Not even for a minute?'

'Why should I? You gave me your word. I'd no reason to think that you wouldn't keep it, or your promise to marry me.' Riquet beamed

broadly, 'I'm so certain, in fact, that I've arranged the wedding.'

The Princess regarded him thoughtfully. 'I'll be frank with you, Riquet. As an intelligent man, I'm sure you'd prefer it.'

'But of course!'

'Well then,' went on the Princess, with an edge to her voice, 'the truth is that I'd forgotten I was to meet you, for I made the promise when I was stupid. And I'm far from certain I can keep my promise to marry you.'

Riquet was completely taken aback. 'B-b-but....' he stammered.

'But what?' said the Princess. 'You knew I wasn't sure about marrying you when I was stupid. If you thought your gift of intelligence would decide me in your favour, you were mistaken. It has made me all the more wary. Nowadays I consider things carefully. I hold back where once I would have rushed in. You might have had a better chance if you'd left me as I was – without a mind of my own or a brain in my head!'

Never had Riquet felt so dismayed and bewildered. His thoughts flew in all directions; for the first time in his life, he was at a loss for words. All his self-possession left him, and the Princess's next words made him feel no happier.

'I know you won't try to bully me over a promise I made as a fool,' she said. 'Only an ignorant brute would say, "You gave your word," and force me to keep it.'

Now Riquet's mind was all knots and tangles. 'But I love you!' he burst out. 'I want to marry you. My happiness depends on it.'

'But you won't force me into marriage because you are not a brute,' said the Princess. 'You're too intelligent to ignore my feelings, too intelligent not to respect them.'

Riquet knew the Princess was right but it gave him no comfort. 'If I were a brute, I could have you for my wife! But it seems I must lose you because I'm intelligent! Is this fair, Princess? Is it reasonable? Intelligence is supposed to be an advantage in life!'

The Princess made no attempt to reply but to Riquet's relief, she didn't walk away. She listened as he desperately pleaded with his voice choked with tears: 'Please tell me, apart from my appearance, do you find anything else about me objectionable? Or abhorrent?'

'No, indeed not!! In all other ways you please me very well!'

Riquet fell to one knee and kissed her hand. 'But if I please you, Princess, your love can make me the most handsome of men!'

Excitedly he reminded her of how the same Fairy, who had given him the power to bestow intelligence on the woman he loved best, had granted her the power to make the man she loved best as beautiful as herself.

'Now that you mention it, I do remember being told something like that,' said the Princess, 'but it was at a time when I was stupid and I must have forgotten it.'

If only he'd asked for her then for the gift of beauty, he would be handsome now, as pleasing to her as she was to him – but he feared that he'd left it too late.

'No, it was I who was stupid,' said Riquet. 'If you can't love me, Princess, it's no more than I deserve.'

At this the Princess smiled and held out her hand: 'If I can make you as handsome as I am beautiful, dear Riquet, then so be it. It is my heart's desire.'

As she spoke, the Princess realised at once she indeed had the power the Fairy had promised! Riquet's ugliness fell away like a discarded cloak. If his eyes squinted, she no longer noticed. She saw only that his eyes were soft with love. If his back was humped, it no longer seemed so: it might bend a little but it was not unbecoming. Even his nose, so large and red that it had repelled her, now seemed admirably heroic.

The more she looked, the more handsome he was to her. There was no question of breaking her promise now, she was now only too pleased to marry him.

The King gladly approved his daughter's decision: 'I left the choice of a husband to you, my daughter, and you have chosen wisely.'

The wedding took place the next day and the newly married couple had not the slightest doubt that they were the happiest couple ever.

SLEEPING BEAUTY

There was once a castle, a very fine castle built of white marble with gold turrets. The turrets of the castle could been seen far and wide across the land. They glittered bright in the sun by day; at night, they shimmered under the moon. From the top of each turret, a brightly-coloured pennant fluttered in the wind.

In the castle lived a King and Queen. They were a light-hearted couple who amused themselves with endless parties, with night-long balls for hundreds of people and other such frivolous pleasures.

But one year, at the same moment of the same day, they decided it was time they had a child. 'We are getting older,' they said, 'and we won't live for ever. We need an heir.'

The years went by and still they had neither a son nor a daughter. In all their lives before, they hadn't suffered a moment's sadness. Now, they knew nothing else! They were filled with such longing for a child that they felt they would die of it.

But at last the Queen gave birth to a daughter. The long-awaited child was so precious that they wanted all the good things of life for her.

'We'll give a banquet,' said the Queen, 'and invite the fairies of the land to bless our daughter with a gift.'

'In return' said King, 'we'll present them with a chest of gold and a golden knife and fork and spoon encrusted with rubies and diamonds.'

Six invitations were sent and six brightly-winged fairies arrived at the banquet. They gathered around the crib where the Princess lay in a robe of white silk and the purest white lace.

The youngest Fairy gave her gift first. 'My gift to the Princess is beauty.'

The next Fairy stepped forward. 'My gift is a mind that is quickwitted and bright.'

'And I give her the power to do whatever she wants with ease,' said the third Fairy.

'Her voice, when she sings, shall be as sweet as a nightingale's,' said the fourth.

'No-one will dance with such grace as the Princess,' said the fifth.

The Eldest Fairy was about to offer her gift but something made her pause. She suddenly turned and everyone followed her gaze. There, standing in the doorway, was an old crone dressed in stone grey with her nails painted grey and grey dusty wings.

She strode up in a rage to the King and Queen. 'Why wasn't I asked to your fine fancy banquet?'

The King and Queen looked at each other in dismay. The Grey Fairy hadn't been seen in their kingdom for years; they'd forgotten all about her.

She read what was in their minds. 'If you'd wanted me here, you'd have remembered me soon enough! You forgot me because you wanted to! You thought an old crone would have nothing to offer your daughter!'

The King and Queen began to stammer their apologies, but the Grey Fairy cut them short.

'Too late! Instead of my gift, your precious Princess shall have my curse.'

Everyone present turned pale and trembled. But no-one dared to speak or to move as the Grey Fairy bent over the Princess, and said: 'A spinning wheel spindle shall prick your hand, my pretty, and you shall die of it!'

With that, the Grey Fairy vanished.

The Queen fainted, the King and the court were in tears. But then the Eldest Fairy stepped forward. 'I have yet to give my gift. I can't remove the Grey Fairy's curse altogether but I can lessen its power. Instead of Death, the eternal sleep, she will sleep for one hundred years and a Prince will wake her with a kiss. Then she shall live her life as she will.'

The King and Queen were greatly relieved. They commanded that all the spinning wheels in the land should be destroyed.

'Now,' they said,' we have nothing to fear from the Grey Fairy's curse, and our daughter can enjoy the gifts that the other fairies have given her.'

They watched as the Princess grew from the most enchanting infant into a beautiful child whom everyone adored. The Grey Fairy's curse faded from memory. By the time the Princess was sixteen, it was all but forgotten, apart from the ban on spinning-wheels.

Just after the Princess's sixteenth birthday party, the King and Queen took themselves off on a holiday to another part of their land.

Left to amuse herself, the Princess decided to explore the castle. 'I'll start at the basement and see what I can find.'

After a while, she found herself in a corridor where she'd never been before. There was a door at the end, so she opened it.

Before her was a spiral staircase with no hand rail. It twisted and turned and was very steep. I hope I don't fall, but I absolutely must find out what's up there, she thought.

Swiftly, not daring to look down, she ran to the top and found herself in the tallest turret of the castle. To her surprise, there was an old woman sitting by the window. Never mind that she was bent and withered and ugly, the Princess gave her a sweet smile and curtsied.

'How do you do, Ma'am. And please, what are you doing?'

The old woman held her hand to her ear, and the Princess repeated the question. 'I'm spinning thread, dear,' the old woman replied.

She was the King's mother's nurse. She'd lived in the turret for so many years, that she'd been forgotten long since. And being deaf, she hadn't heard about the ban on spinning wheels.

Never having seen one before, the Princess was curious. 'I'd like to spin like you. Please may I try?'

The old nurse got up from the stool, and the Princess took her place. Never having used a spinning wheel before, her hand fumbled and the spindle pricked her finger. She gave a soft cry and fell at once to the floor.

The old nurse thought she had fainted and gave the alarm. By the time the King and Queen arrived, however, the Princess's heartbeat had faded to the faintest flutter. 'She is dying!' they cried, half mad with grief.

It was a dwarf who reminded them of the Eldest Fairy's gift. He had magic shoes that carried him to her palace in a trice.

A moment later the Eldest Fairy arrived in a chariot of fire drawn by fire-breathing dragons. She bent over the Princess and breathed life into her. 'Now she will sleep for a hundred years until the Prince's kiss wakes her. And when she wakes, she shall find her court about her.'

The Eldest Fairy went about the castle and touched the butlers and maids and the courtiers and even the guard dogs with her wand; they too fell asleep in an instant.

'But what about us?' cried the King and Queen. 'We're her parents. We're the ones who should be there when she wakes!'

'Alas,' said the Eldest Fairy, 'that cannot be.'

The King and Queen comforted themselves that at least their daughter would find some familiar faces around her when she woke. They carried her to a bed hung with curtains threaded with silk and gold. Then they left the castle, commanding that no one should go near it until she woke.

'You need have no fear on that account,' said the Eldest Fairy.

She sent a command to the trees and creepers that lay beneath the earth. At once they burst through the ground and formed a forest about the castle so that it was hidden from view and only the gold turrets could be seen rising above. Within, the Princess and the court slept.

The years rolled by. In the course of time the King and Queen died and a new family ruled the land. The Princess was forgotten, and rumours spread about the ever deepening forest. It was said that an ogre lived there who would eat alive anyone who ventured within.

The new royal family lived in a large palace in the city. But one day the Prince came riding with his court into the country, seeking excitement and adventure.

'This forest intrigues me,' he said. 'I'm curious to explore it.'

The courtiers began to explain about the ogre. Then an old man stepped forward and doffed his cap to the Prince. 'Don't you go believing them, Sir. There's no ogre in there. My mother told me so. And no word of a lie passed her lips in all her life, God rest her soul.'

'You're just a peasant!' the courtiers jeered. 'What would you know! Or your old mother either!'

'That will do!' rapped out the Prince. He bowed courteously to the old man and asked him what his mother had told him.

'What she told me was this, Sir. Beneath those gold turrets is a castle. And in the castle lives a Princess. And no ordinary Princess either! But the fairest in all the world, blessed by the six good fairies of the land.'

At this, the Prince felt a rapid fluttering in his heart. He wanted to hear more about the Princess but, when he looked again, the old man had gone.

Perhaps he's a creature of the ogre, he thought, out to trick me into entering the forest. But on the other hand, if a Princess lived there – what a prize she would be!

Before his courage escaped him, he urged his horse forward. His courtiers refused to follow. 'Then I'll go alone,' said the Prince.

The deeper he went into the forest, the more thickly the trees grew. He had to abandon his horse and make his way on foot. About him echoed strange cries of unseen creatures. Shadows rose up all around and the Prince no longer knew whether it was night or day. But he pressed on until he reached the huge door of a castle. Two sharp-toothed dogs guarded it. He took one slow step forward, then another, but they didn't even stir. Thankfully he stepped over them. Now he was in the castle.

In fear and trembling at what he would find there, he went from room to room. The dust of a hundred years lay everywhere, and when he saw the sleeping courtiers, silent and still as death, he feared that at any moment death would strike him as well.

At last he came to the Princess's bedroom. Here there was no dust and the air was fresh. He approached the bed and drew the curtains. There lay the Princess, with the flush of roses on her cheek and the gold of corn in her hair. He saw the pulse rise and fall in her throat and knew that she wasn't dead, but only sleeping.

The Prince drew closer. And the closer he came, the more beautiful she seemed. Her lips were slightly parted. He longed to kiss her. He glanced quickly over his shoulder. No one would know if he stole a kiss, just one....

As soon as his lips touched hers, the Princess woke. The Prince drew back, ashamed. But at that moment the court woke also and came rushing to the Princess. They explained about the hundred year's sleep, from which a Prince would wake her with a kiss.

Now his secret was out! The Prince fell at once on his knees, and begged the Princess to marry him. 'I know that I shall love no one, my Sleeping Beauty, as I love you.'

Sleeping Beauty, as he called her, smiled. For her too, it was love at first sight. She took his hand. 'And I shall love no other but you.'

They decided then and there to be married without delay, and they were married before the day was out.

The next morning, the Prince woke early. 'I have business to attend to,' he told Sleeping Beauty. 'I'll be back at nightfall.'

Swiftly he rode to his parents' palace. They'd heard he'd gone to explore the forest and were relieved to see him.

'We've been worried, my son,' said the King.

'Tell me, My Own,' said the Queen, 'just what did you find in this forest?'

The Prince shrugged. 'Just an old castle. Nothing of interest.'

The Queen smoothed his brow. 'You've been away three days and nights. You must be tired and hungry, My Love.'

'No, not at all,' said the Prince. Then he quickly added, 'I met an old charcoal burner. He gave me a bed of sweet straw to sleep on and fed me handsomely on bread and cheese.'

He was bursting to tell them the truth, to tell them about Sleeping Beauty. His father, he thought, would be pleased. But his mother?

Although she looked like an ordinary woman, this was just a disguise. The Queen came from a race of ogresses whose favourite food was the flesh of young children. She knew the King had only married her for her vast wealth. Afraid that otherwise he would leave her, she was careful to keep her ogress nature in check; even so, when a child came within reach, it was all she could do to stop herself gobbling it up.

The Prince knew his mother was an ogress. He loved her despite it, but he was also afraid of her. He dreaded to think what she'd do if she found out that he'd got secretly married!

So when dusk fell he told his parents, 'I'm going hunting. I'll be back in the morning.'

Every night the Prince returned to Sleeping Beauty. To his relief, never once did she ask, Where have you been all day? She lived in a glow, in a daze of love for him and their children. The first was a daughter, called Dawn. Then followed a son they called Day.

As for his parents – his father swallowed the hunting story but his mother wasn't so sure! She was always asking him why he went hunting at night when he never caught anything!

But the Prince would answer her with a dazzling smile and a kiss, and she'd cease her questions until the next time.

After two years, his father died. The Queen became the Dowager Queen and the Prince became King. I'm my own master, and I shall bring Sleeping Beauty and her children to the palace to live with me, he decided.

To his surprise, his mother didn't get into a rage. She welcomed Sleeping Beauty like an honoured guest and wouldn't let her do a thing. As for

the children, Princess Dawn and Prince Day, they'd only to ask for a new toy or whatever and she'd say, 'You shall have it, my little darlings.'

Even if they were naughty, she wouldn't scold them. 'Scolded children grow tiresome and tough. But spoil them, and they'll grow the sweeter!'

The Prince, now King, was delighted. 'How splendid,' he said, 'that we're all so happy together.'

But then danger threatened his kingdom. His neighbour, the fierce warrior Emperor Cantabutte, threatened to invade it. 'I shall have to fight him,' he told Sleeping Beauty. 'But never fear, I'll return safely. And while I'm away, you'll have nothing to worry you. My mother shall rule the kingdom, and look after you and our children.'

And so saying, the King departed.

Sleeping Beauty had been living at the palace for a couple of years. But this was the first time the Dowager Queen had been alone with her. The

next morning she ordered Sleeping Beauty to go to the country, where she had a house in the depths of a wood.

Sleeping Beauty protested. 'I'd rather stay here, Ma'am.'

'Who has the King left in charge? You or me? Now get going, and take your brats with you!'

Wondering why the Dowager Queen was suddenly so sharp with her, Sleeping Beauty set off for the country.

Eight days later the Dowager Queen arrived at the country house. She summoned the young clerk who was in charge of the kitchens. 'I want to order tomorrow's dinner,' she said.

'What would you like, Ma'am?' the young clerk enquired.

The Dowager Queen began to laugh. In terror, the clerk saw her disguise fall away and before him stood an ogress with eyes that were hard as flint.

'For my dinner tomorrow,' she said, in a voice that was soft, but which chilled his blood, 'I shall eat the Princess Dawn.'

The clerk turned white. But the ogress was plainly in no mood to argue, and the next morning he went to the nursery with a large knife.

Princess Dawn came running up and flung her arms about him. 'Have you brought me some candy?' she asked.

The clerk faltered. 'The child is all innocence. I cannot kill her.'

He dropped his knife and carried the Princess to the far end of the courtyard where he lived with his wife. He told his wife to hide her.

'I'll kill a lamb,' he said, 'and serve that in her place. If I make a sauce that is thick and spicy, hopefully the ogress won't notice the difference!'

'Tasty, very tasty,' said the ogress Queen, as she tore with her teeth at the lamb's flesh, thinking it was Princess Dawn. But even more she relished Sleeping Beauty's despair when she discovered her daughter was missing.

'My daughter has been stolen! I fear she is dead,' wept Sleeping Beauty. 'I have failed to protect my own daughter.'

The clerk longed to tell her that the Princess was alive, but he was too afraid. He was relieved when the Dowager Queen returned to the city.

Eight days passed, and the Dowager Queen returned again to the country. Once more, she sent for the clerk. 'For my supper, I fancy a juicy little boy. Sleeping Beauty's second child, Prince Day, will do very nicely.'

The clerk hurried to the nursery. He found the boy pretending to fence with his pet monkey. This time he didn't hesitate. He took the Prince quickly home to his wife, then killed a young goat and served it to the ogress with a thick, spicy sauce. She swallowed the meal at a gulp, then hurried off to the nursery to find Sleeping Beauty half-crazed with grief.

'My son has been stolen, like my daughter before him! I'm the wretchedest mother in all the world and my husband will despise me,' she wept despairingly.

The Dowager Queen was all sympathy – but inwardly she was gloating. The clerk stood by helplessly and said nothing.

He watched thankfully as the ogress departed once more for the city. The clerk thought he'd seen the last of her – so far as the ogress knew, she'd eaten both Sleeping Beauty's children. But after another eight days, she came back and he was summoned again.

'I've not eaten all week! I've been saving myself for someone – or should I say someone – I've been wanting to eat for a long time! Bring me Little Miss Pretty Face!' roared the ogress. 'Go at once and fetch me my dinner!'

The clerk was in despair. 'If I don't do as she she says, she'll eat me instead! It's my life, or Sleeping Beauty's.'

The clerk took his dagger and went to her chamber. I shan't take her life unawares, I shall tell her the truth, he decided.

When he told Sleeping Beauty that the ogress Queen had sent him to kill her, he expected her at least to weep. But she didn't. She just sat very still, as if frozen.

At last she said, 'Did she tell you to kill my children also?'

The clerk nodded and before he could say anything further, Sleeping Beauty went on, 'The sooner I die, the sooner I shall see my children again.' She lowered her head and told the clerk to strike.

He raised the dagger. But at the sight of her neck so white and smooth bared before him, he fell to his knees and wept. 'So help me, even though it cost me my life, you shall both live and see your children!'

He took Sleeping Beauty home. And no sooner had he done so, than he saw a doe at the edge of the wood. Quickly he killed it, then he served it to the ogress, careful to ensure the sauce was both very thick and very spicy.

She crunched her way through the last of the bones and licked her lips. 'That's the most agreeable meal, I've had! And now I shall prepare for the King's return.'

But as she was crossing the courtyard, she heard the sound of a child crying. It seemed to come from the clerk's house. She knew he had no children and curious, she peered in through the window.

What she saw was this:

Princess Dawn tugging at her mother's skirt, and begging her not to be cross with her brother, who'd been especially naughty.

'Please don't be angry, Mama. He won't be naughty again,' the Princess pleaded.

Realising she had been cheated, in a fury the ogress ordered that a huge tub should be filled with poisonous snakes and toads. Then Sleeping Beauty, her children, the clerk and his wife were brought into the kitchen with their hands tightly bound. The ogress turned to the executioners. 'Throw them in!' she commanded.

But at that moment the King burst into the kitchen. Having conquered the Emperor, he'd been filled with such longing to see Sleeping Beauty and his children again, he'd ridden at full speed from the battlefield to find them, arriving sooner than his mother had expected.

In horror, he gazed at the sight before him. 'What's going on? What's the meaning of this?'

No one dared answer, for the ogress Queen held them silent with a terrifying gaze.

The King looked towards his mother, angry and questioning. 'I demand an answer at once.'

The ogress gave a cry that shook the house and the roots of the trees. All her plotting and planning had come to nothing! Another cry, and she hurled herself into the tub and was devoured by the creatures within.

The only person who mourned for her was the King; she was after all his mother.

Then he turned to Sleeping Beauty. 'But I am blessed in you, my Queen, the dearest wife in all the world, and in our son and daughter.'

From then on, it is said, the King and Queen lived happily ever after.

THE THREE WISHES

A woodcutter sat under a tree. His name was Blaise and he felt so weighed down with despair he put his head in his hands and moaned and groaned out loud.

'My life is work, work, work, with little to show for it. I'm always wishing for something better but the gods don't listen! They grant other people's wishes not mine, oh no! I'd sooner be dead than go on as I am!'

His words reached the mighty god, Zeus, who ruled the world. He came swooping down from the sky with a thunderbolt in one hand.

The terrified Blaise threw himself to the ground. 'Forgive me, O Zeus! I didn't mean to complain. Never mind about my wishes, just spare me your thunderbolt and let me stay as I am.'

'You've no cause to be frightened,' said the almighty god Zeus. 'I heard what you say, and I've come to show you your complaint is unjust. I grant you three wishes. You may wish for whatever you choose. Now is your chance to make yourself happy. But remember,' he added, 'your happiness will depend on what you wish for. So think carefully before you make the wishes.'

'I will, Lord Zeus, you can be sure of that ! Thank you, Your Mightiness!'

The god vanished into the sky and Blaise ran quickly home to his wife. I must discuss with my missus such an important matter as this, he thought.

His wife was called Fanchon. She was a lively, clever girl, and pretty too. As Blaise told her about the three wishes, at once she thought of a thousand things – grand and wonderful things – that they could wish for.

'But it's best to be prudent and think things over. Let's sleep on it Blaise, love,' she said, 'and make our first wish tomorrow.'

'Good thinking, sweetheart! But in the meantime,' said Blaise, 'let's have some wine to celebrate! Our worries and cares are over and now we can live as we please.'

He drew his chair up by the fire. 'This is more like it! A glass of wine and a good blaze in the grate. Do you know what I wish I had? A mile of black pudding would go down a treat!'

The words were no sooner out of his mouth than his wife saw a black pudding slide down the chimney, then come wriggling like a snake towards her. She opened her lungs and screamed: 'AAAAAH!'

Then she realised: 'It's your wishing what's done it, you Clod, you Ninny, you Big Daft Cabbage! You could have wished us an empire, gold and pearls and rubies and diamonds and fancy clothes! But no! You wished for a black pudding.'

'All right, I made a boob,' muttered her husband. 'No need to go on about it. I've still got two wishes left.'

'And I dare say you'll waste them as well!' shrieked his wife. 'You oaf! You ox! You… you… Thick-headed Stupid!'

Blaise turned on her angrily. 'I'd be better off without a wife than one like you! A plague on you, Wife, and the pudding! I wish to Zeus it was stuck on your nose!'

The wish was instantly granted!

Fanchon looked in the mirror in horror! The great black pudding hung down over her mouth so she could hardly open it to speak.

I shan't complain about that, thought Blaise. I've one wish left and I could wish myself a King. But what sort of King would I be, he pondered, with a Queen that has a mile of black pudding stuck on her nose? I'd best ask herself what she thinks in the matter.

'Now, Fanchon,' he said, 'here's a question: would you rather be a Queen with a black pudding nose or be a woodcutter's wife with the sweet nose that you had!'

Fanchon considered. If she were a Queen no one would dare to remark on her nose! But on the other hand, she liked being pretty and at last

she decided she'd sooner keep her looks and remain a peasant than be an ugly Queen.

'That's my thinking also,' said Blaise. 'I hereby wish my missus was as she was. Besides,' he added, 'who wants to be King? Better by far to make do as I am.'

Up above on his throne the mighty god Zeus smiled down at the woodcutter who could have had all the abundance of heaven and earth, but who could wish for no more than to stay just as he was.

THE TALE
OF TOM THUMB

In the days of giants and ogres and other monster-like men, life for the poor was a struggle. It was those who had no land of their own who suffered most; every morning they'd wake to find themselves face to face with hunger or cold or both.

There was a woodcutter and his wife who were as poor as any and they had seven children to keep. All but the last were twins. The last to arrive was so small and so skinny his father declared: 'This wee chappie's no bigger than my thumb!' After that, everyone called him Tom Thumb.

His parents waited for him to grow as their other children before him. He did grow, but only very slowly; for his age he remained quite exceptionally small. What's more, while the twins were soon chattering like monkeys, their Tom Thumb was slow in speaking. But he did a great deal of listening.

'He mightn't say much,' said his parents, 'but maybe he's no more the fool for that!'

Their large family meant the woodcutter and his wife had to work hard to keep a roof over their heads and enough food in their tummies to keep them from starving.

But then a famine struck the land when the crops failed. Only the rich could afford such food as there was. The woodcutter and his wife were in despair.

'One thing I can't bear above all others, and that is to watch and wait for my children to starve!' said the woodcutter.

His wife agreed, 'But what else can we do?'

'I'll take the children to the forest,' he told her. 'I'll leave them there, and let them take their chance.'

'You'd never do such a thing!' cried his horrified wife. 'And if you did, you'd soon regret it!'

'Better than to watch them starve. For sure as fate, that's what will happen if they stay here.'

The woodcutter's wife couldn't argue with that. 'But to abandon our little darlings in the depths of the forest,' she wept. 'They will be eaten by wolves, or fall into a bog and drown. It will break my heart and yours too.'

But the woodcutter kept arguing and at last his wife was persuaded that the children might somehow survive in the forest, whereas only death awaited them at home. They decided it must be done the next morning.

Not for a minute did his parents guess that Tom Thumb was listening to every word! When the woodcutter had said to his wife, 'I want to talk about the children,' Tom Thumb had crept out of bed and into the room and then, unnoticed, crept over the floor and under his father's chair.

He waited until his parents had gone to bed. Then Tom Thumb slipped out of doors and gathered a pocketful of white pebbles that gleamed beneath the moon. The next morning as his father led them away, Tom Thumb lagged behind and dropped the pebbles to mark the way.

As the sun rose high, the woodcutter decided he'd come far enough. He sent the children off to collect firewood. With a heart heavy as lead, he slipped away and headed for home.

When they realised they were alone, that their father had left them, the three pairs of twins wept and wailed: 'When night comes, the wolves will smell us and eat us!'

But Tom Thumb reassured them. 'I know the way home. Follow me.'

The pebbles guided them back through the forest. But as they reached the door, the children paused. From inside they heard shouts, very loud shouts! Their parents were having a row, and they didn't want to go in!

What had happened was this…. After the woodcutter had left his children to their fate in the forest, he had arrived home to find the last thing in the world he'd expected: on the kitchen table were ten gold coins.

'It's the money the Mayor was owing,' said his wife. 'We'd quite despaired of him paying his debt. But now thanks be praised, he's paid up!'

Their first thought was to fill their aching bellies, and so they bought food and wine. But when they'd eaten as much as they could, the wife's thoughts turned to their children.

'There's more than enough food left over to have fed the poor mites. But now it's too late! Either they'll have frozen to death in the night cold or wolves will have eaten them. Oh what wicked parents we are! Why did we ever do such a thing. I told you we shouldn't. I said we'd regret it!'

'Yes, yes, I know,' said the woodcutter.

His wife went on and on, 'I told you so. I knew we'd regret it.'

'That's enough! It's done!'

The woodcutter shouted so loudly the walls of their humble cottage trembled, and his wife began to weep.

'My children! My darlings! I'll never see them again!'

The children could bear their mother's grief no longer. They burst in through the door. 'Here we are, Mother! Safe and sound!'

What joy there was! What kissing and hugging! Their mother sat the children down at the table and their parents looked on with delight as the children feasted.

Their happiness lasted as long as the money. When the last coin was spent, hunger cursed the family once more, and the woodcutter and his wife were filled with despair.

The woodcutter found it no easier than before to watch his children starving for want of food.

'I shall take them to the forest, sooner than that!'

'They'll find their way home again! retorted his wife.

'This time I shall take them so deep in the forest, they'll not find the path back. They'll have to find their own way to wherever it takes them!'

'And I know where that is! Into the mouths of the wolves!'

'Be that as it may, there's only death for them here,' said the woodcutter.

At last his wife agreed: awful as it was for her hungry children, the forest was the lesser of two terrible evils.

But Tom Thumb, alert as ever, had heard what was decided. Once more he waited until his parents had gone to bed. Once more he went downstairs, thinking to collect pebbles to mark the way as before. But he found the door locked and bolted.

But he didn't panic: Tom Thumb was well used to danger. Every day, every minute, he had to keep his wits about him just to stay alive! Otherwise, he'd have been squashed like a fly by the big clumsy feet of his brothers and sisters long since. Accidentally of course, but that was no comfort when one was squashed flat! Many a time, he'd jumped out of the way of a hovering foot and saved his skin by a whisker.

If I keep my head, I'll find a way round this too, thought Tom Thumb. And so it proved!

The next morning, their Father said, 'Come along, children. We're going to collect wood from the forest.'

Their mother, red-eyed and weeping, gave each child a crust of bread, the last that she had.

The other children ate theirs quickly. But not Tom Thumb. He broke the crust into little bits and dropped the pieces along the path as markers.

This time the woodcutter waited until the sun was setting before he gave his children the slip, then he hurried off home.

As soon as they realised they'd been abandoned in the dark, in the cold of the night, the three pairs of twins were filled with terror.

'Cheer up,' said Tom Thumb. 'I'll find the way home.'

But when he looked for the markers, they were gone: the birds had eaten the crumbs.

For a moment, Tom Thumb shivered with fear. But the trees were tall and he thought, if I climb to the top of the tallest, maybe from there I'll see somewhere to shelter.

His small size was a help in clambering up to the top of the tree. His weight didn't break the branches and from the tipmost top he could see far and wide over the forest. In the distance he saw a light shimmer. It must be a candle, he thought. And a candle means a home and a home means people!

When he was back on the ground, the candle was lost from view. 'Never mind,' he said to the others, 'I think it was that way.'

Although he was a fraction their size, Tom Thumb walked in front and the others followed. Soon they saw the candle lighting the dark, and then the outline of a cottage.

Weary but thankful they ran towards it. Not for a minute did they guess that the cottage belonged to an ogre! Luckily he was out, and his wife opened the door.

'Mistress, please let us in!' begged Tom Thumb. 'Otherwise the cold of the night will freeze us to death or the wolves will eat us!'

'Oh my! What shall I do?' cried the ogre's wife.

She knew her husband only too well. There was nothing he liked better than young children's flesh and when he came home he was sure to kill and eat them.

But she didn't want to frighten the children by telling them that! Nor could she leave them to the cold or the wolves. 'Come on in,' she said.

She warmed them by the fire and fed them.

'Now get under the bed and stay there until my husband goes out in the morning.'

A moment later her husband burst in through the door, 'Wife, wife, where's my dinner!'

'Just coming!' she answered quickly.

His wife took a sheep from the spit and put it on the table before him. It was scarcely cooked, the blood was still running, but that was how the ogre liked it. He tore at the flesh with his big ogre's teeth.

Then he paused – and sniffed. 'I smell living flesh!' said the ogre.

'It must be the sheep,' said his wife.

'This sheep's as dead as a dodo. I know what I can smell and I know that I'm right.'

His nose led him towards the bed. He looked underneath it and found Tom Thumb and his sisters and brothers.

'You tried to deceive me, wife!' he roared.

His wife stammered, 'I…I…I thought as you had the sheep for your dinner, you'd be satisfied with that.'

'Did you indeed! Well, I fancy these tender young morsels!'

The ogre took out his knife. But his wife was quick-thinking: 'You've got the sheep to finish. And I've also prepared a pig and a deer for you. Best not let them to go to waste. Why not save the children for tomorrow?'

The ogre nodded. 'There's some sense in that.'

Before he could change his mind, the ogre's wife told Tom Thumb and the children to follow her. She led them upstairs to a large bedroom with two big beds in it.

In one of the beds seven girls were sleeping. They were the ogre's young daughters and they each wore a nightcap held in place by a circlet of gold. Asleep, they looked innocent enough. But they had more of their father's blood in their veins than their mother's. As yet they hadn't eaten human flesh, but it wouldn't be long before they started. Already they used their sharp little teeth to bite other children and suck out their blood.

The second bed, however, was empty. 'Quickly, get in,' said the ogre's wife. 'Now I must tend to my husband.'

After their meal and in the warmth of the bed, his brothers and sisters were soon asleep. But Tom Thumb stayed awake. He didn't trust the ogre at all. He didn't trust him not to change his mind and to kill them before the night was out.

'I led my brothers and sisters here. It's up to me to get them out alive. Whatever the cost, I will not flinch. I'll do it!' vowed Tom Thumb.

Stealthily he slid out of the bed and removed the nightcaps and the circlets of gold from the sleeping girls. Keeping one for himself, he put the others on his brothers and and sisters. Then he waited. And waited.

He heard the ogre and his wife go to bed.

He heard the ogre get out of his bed, and come down the passage.

He heard the door open.

He saw the shadow of the ogre and the raised knife.

'I don't believe in taking chances. Strike while the iron is hot, that's my motto! Best to kill the children now,' muttered the ogre. 'Tomorrow they might escape. Tomorrow someone might save them! Or another ogre might steal them away!'

He bent over the first bed he came to and quickly drew back as his hand touched a circlet of gold. Then he felt another and another, seven in fact.

'That was a narrow escape! I almost killed my own daughters,' he muttered.

He moved to the next bed. This time he didn't hesitate. He cut the throats of the sleeping children, not knowing they were his daughters. Then he went back to bed.

As soon as the ogre had gone, Tom Thumb woke his brothers and sisters. 'Come quickly, quietly, at once! We must flee!'

Light of foot and swift as the wind, they ran off through the forest. They ran and they ran.

The next morning the ogre sat down to breakfast. He waited for his daughters. When they didn't come down, he went up to fetch them.

As soon as he opened the bedroom door, he realised what had happened. He let out a howl of anguish and rage, then shouted, 'Fetch me my seven-league boots!'

His wife was so distressed at what her husband had unwittingly done to their daughters, that she could scarcely see for weeping. But she fetched his magic boots and he put them on. Then he stormed out of the house to search for Tom Thumb and his brothers and sisters.

'I'll hunt them down and eat them alive!' shrieked the ogre.

He was in such a state of anger and torment, he didn't think where he was going. He went aimlessly this way and that, striding over rivers and mountains through the magic of the boots.

About midday, he was heading towards Tom Thumb and his brothers and sisters who, to their grateful surprise, had found themselves within striking distance of home. But before they could reach it, they saw the ogre.

'Quickly, hide in this cave,' commanded Tom Thumb.

The ogre now was almost upon them. But he didn't know he was so close to his prey, and so he sat down to rest. The seven-league boots enabled him to take great strides and cover huge distances very quickly, but at a price: they ate up his strength and made him extraordinarily weary.

His head sank on to his chest and soon his thunderous snores rang through the forest shaking the trees.

'Go home! Hurry!' Tom Thumb urged his brothers and sisters.

'What about you?'

'Don't worry about me! I know what I'm going to do! And I shall succeed!'

The twins did as he'd said, and Tom Thumb crept up to the sleeping ogre. Being so small, he made no sound. His little fingers were light and nimble; the ogre didn't stir as Tom Thumb unlaced the seven-league boots.

Now for the next part of his plan. Small he might be, but Tom Thumb's will gave him the strength of ten full-sized men! One! Two! He pulled the boots off the huge feet and put them on his own.

The seven-league boots had such magic within, they shrank at once to fit Tom Thumb's small feet. In a couple of strides, he stepped over the forest to the ogre's cottage.

'Mistress, I bring news of your husband,' he said.

He told the ogre's wife that her husband had been kidnapped by bandits. In return for his safe return, they demanded all the gold and everything of value that they possessed.

The wife didn't hesitate. Her husband was an ogre, yes. But in his own ogre-like way he loved her, and she couldn't let him be killed by bandits.

She gave Tom Thumb the sack of gold under the floorboards, the gold-painted china, the gold knives and forks and spoons, everything of value she could lay her hands on. With a mighty feat of will, he picked up the lot. But it was a mere step or two home in his seven-league boots, and somehow he managed it.

When the ogre woke and found his seven-league boots had been stolen, he limped back through the forest, too broken by grief at what he'd done to his daughters to search for the thief. When he got home and realised that he'd been tricked once more by a lad who stood lower than his knee, he sank even deeper into depression. His wife tried to comfort him, but she too was weakened by grief. From that time on, each day dawned grimly for them both.

As for Tom Thumb and his family, how they prospered! With the ogre's gold, his Father bought land to plant and harvest, and they were never cold or hungry again. The twins grew up and had children of their own. Tom Thumb, however, never married, nor did he grow any taller. But he was much loved by his horde of nieces and nephews.

'If it wasn't for you, Uncle, we wouldn't be here! Our Ma's and our Pa's would have been eaten up by the ogre!'

'Maybe not, maybe so!' said Uncle Tom Thumb.